POINT BLANK

POINT BLANK

THE SILENCER SERIES BOOK 5

MIKE RYAN

WWW.MIKERYANBOOKS.COM

1

———

Recker was sitting on an oversized chair in a dark corner of the living room, waiting for his target to come home. The lack of light disguised his presence. Now that he knew the man's wife and two young kids would not be home, Recker no longer had to wait for the right opportunity to come along. After a brief stay in the hospital, the wife texted her husband she was taking the kids to her parents' house for a couple of days. It would take a little longer, though, for the bruises to go away.

Teresa Golden had been abused by her husband for at least a year from what Jones could figure out. It wasn't until this last time she had to go to the hospital for treatment. Though she told everyone she fell down the stairs, it was quite obvious it wasn't the case. Jones first got wind of her problem several weeks earlier when his software program picked up a text from Golden to her sister, saying her husband had hit her. With children at the ages of nine and six, Recker wanted to take Richard Golden out permanently, fearful the abuse he unleashed on his wife would eventually spill over to their children. Jones, though, successfully debated that the loss of their father at such a young age would be devastating to them and made Recker reluctantly agree to his partner's plans. Jones argued he could continue to monitor the situation to make sure the kids were never harmed. Recker wasn't so sure Jones would be able to tell and the kids' case wouldn't get lost eventually under the sea of assignments they were likely to get in the coming months. Plus, Jones had convinced his partner he had to change his ways of handling things or else they'd always have to wind up moving after a few years. They had to start working towards handling killing as a final option and not the first choice.

Recker wasn't very fond of their newfound way of doing things, but he was willing to try it for a while. At least until he proved to Jones it wasn't working, which he suspected would be relatively soon. In the case of Teresa Golden, Jones hoped just working her husband over would be enough to scare him by letting him know he was being watched. Recker didn't believe it would work though. He feared giving Richard Golden some bruises of his own, would only make the man angrier and worse, thinking his wife had something to do with it and told someone about him.

Recker didn't particularly care for this less violent and

friendlier, at least in his mind, version of himself. It'd been a long time since he pulled the trigger with a target standing in front of him, and while he still didn't enjoy it, he still believed it was as necessary as ever with some people. No matter what Jones said, or how he explained it, or how it benefited them by keeping their profile lower, Recker would never be convinced some people could be rehabilitated or scared into better behavior. Some people just had to be dealt with by violence. It's just the way it was.

Regardless of his own personal views, Recker was playing Jones' game for the moment. He'd been waiting in the Golden home for about an hour in anticipation of Richard Golden getting home from the bar, his usual stop every Friday after work. Recker was staring against the far wall at a big bow window, looking into the dark night air through an open slit of the brown curtains. He'd just taken his phone out to look at the time when he noticed a bright flash before a pair of steady car lights shone through the windows. He slowly put the phone back in his pocket as he calmly waited for his victim to walk through the door.

Recker heard the metal juggling of keys as they clanged against each other as Golden tried to steady his hand to unlock the front door. He could already tell Golden wouldn't be much of a problem. Judging by how long it took the man to open the door, Recker felt confident his target already had too much to drink. He was soon proven right as he watched Golden stumble his way into the house. Golden staggered his way into the living room and flicked on the lights via the switch on the wall. He did a double take and took a step backward, not sure if he was seeing correctly or if he was more under the influence of alcohol than he thought. He shook his head to shake off the effects of the booze as if it would suddenly make the man sitting in his living room go away. Once Golden realized his vision wasn't going away, he wiped the sweat from his hands off on his shirt, then his pants. He moved slightly to his right as he steadied himself on the back of a nearby chair, looking uncomfortable in the presence of a stranger in his home.

"Who the hell are you?"

"I'm uh, just a concerned citizen," Recker said.

"Get out of my house before I call the police."

"I think that would be a mistake on your part. Or if you'd like, we can wait until they get here and we can exchange stories. You can tell them how I broke into your house, I can tell them how much you've beaten up on your wife over the past few months, including her hospital trip yesterday."

Golden looked stunned that his visitor knew about his misdeeds.

"So, who are you and what do you want?"

"I told you, I'm just a concerned third party," Recker said.

"Did my wife put you up to this?"

"No, I come from an organization that oversees matters like this. We watch from a distance," Recker said, standing up.

As Golden watched his visitor get up from his chair, a lump went down his throat in anticipation of what the man might do to him. Recker never had a pleasant look on his face when he was on an assignment and he looked even more intimidating to someone whose mind was in a haze. Recker took a few steps toward his impending victim, causing Golden to panic. He ran back into the hallway, racing up the steps to get to his son's room, though in his condition it was more like stumbling up the stairs. Recker followed his target, though in no apparent hurry to inflict the damage he was about to unleash. He slowly and methodically walked up the stairs, knowing Golden wasn't in a state where he could easily slip away from him. And Recker wouldn't have even feared him if Golden's mind was clear, let alone in the alcohol infested haze he was in. But even though Recker didn't fear the man, it didn't mean he wasn't alert. Anybody could get in a lucky shot if he wasn't being careful or took his opponent for granted.

As Recker reached the top step, he was bracing himself for a surprise attack. As soon as both feet were on the second floor, he looked in both directions, not sure which way Golden went. As he looked to his right, he saw movement out of the corner of his eye. It was almost like a blur coming toward him, though Recker ducked just in time as he saw the baseball bat swinging at him. The bat shattered pieces of the corner of the drywall, plaster falling onto the floor. Once Recker rose up after the bat whiffed past him, he countered Golden's assault with a thunderous left hand across the cheek of the drunken man's face. Hurt from the blow, Golden staggered into the wall, unable to counter with an offensive of his own. With his target seemingly stuck to the wall, Recker moved in and alternated between his right and left hand across both sides of Golden's face in a furious fashion. Once Golden put his hands up to guard the onslaught across his face, Recker turned his attention a little lower. He gave Golden a few shots to his midsection, knocking the wind out of him and causing him to hunch over. As his victim crossed his arms and clutched at his stomach, Recker looked down and saw the baseball bat lying there. He picked up the wooden weapon with his left hand then cocked his right hand in order to deliver a vicious uppercut to Golden's jaw. The back of Golden's head smacked into the wall, putting a slight indentation into the drywall, and giving him an even bigger headache. As he put his hands against his chin, Recker grabbed the handle of the bat with both hands and swung at Golden's stomach. The man instantly fell to his knees as he struggled to breathe, feeling his ribs crushed by the blow. As Golden was on the ground on all fours, he began spitting out blood as he gasped for air.

In the heat of the moment, Recker's first inclination was to keep the punishment raining down onto Golden's body. He took a firm handle of the bat once more and waved it over his head, ready to deliver at least one more blow to the back of Golden's head, possibly a fatal one. But before he swung down, Recker thought of Jones' words to him, about trying to turn over a new leaf. As he looked down at his victim, unsure what to do, some of the rage inside Recker's body slowly evaporated. He took a deep breath and tried to compose himself. He slowly brought the bat down and held it with one hand at his side before he let it slip away from his fingers as it knocked around on the laminate flooring.

Figuring his time there was done, Recker delivered a final message by kicking Golden once more in the midsection. The blow caused him to crumple to the ground in agony. As he lay there on the floor, writhing in pain, moaning amongst the coughing and blood-spitting, Recker squatted to give him some lasting words to remember him by.

"This was just a little warm-up," Recker said. "In the coming weeks and months, I'll be keeping an eye on things. You'll never see me or know when I'm near. But if I hear you have laid another hand on your wife or kids, I'll be back. And I guarantee I won't be nearly as friendly as I've been tonight."

Recker stood back up and adjusted his clothes before taking a final look at his victim on the ground. He calmly walked back down the steps as if nothing had ever happened, without a care in the world. He continued right out the front door and into his car, driving away with the satisfaction from successfully completing another assignment, even if it wasn't quite to the level he would have liked.

Six months had gone by since Recker and Jones had relocated to Michigan. Instead of living inside the city limits of Detroit, they set up shop in the suburbs, just as they had done in Philadelphia. Dearborn was the city Jones had chosen. Located in Wayne County and part of the Detroit metropolitan area, Dearborn was one of the larger cities in the state and also the home of Ford headquarters. Their operation worked so well in Philly that Jones sought to replicate everything almost entirely in their new home, right down to the office setup. The only difference for the professor was, instead of getting his own apartment, he lived right there in the office. This one was a little larger than their previous one, with an extra room off of the main quarters. It was supposed to be for another small office but Jones turned it into a bedroom with a foldout couch which turned into a bed. Considering he spent most of his time in the office anyway, it didn't seem worthwhile to him to get his own place. With the couch, a TV, and a small table, it was all he needed. The bathroom had a small shower, and they kept a large refrigerator in the main office, so it contained all the comforts of home for him.

Recker, on the other hand, made a few minor changes from how he approached things in Philadelphia. Though he did get another small apartment as he did before, that was it. He didn't attempt to get to know any other players in town like he did with Vincent and Jeremiah, didn't try to establish any contacts the way he did with Tyrell, and he didn't make friends with anyone like Mia. He felt the risks outweighed the benefits in trying to do the same in Detroit. Plus, he just wasn't interested in complicating relationships the way they once were. Recker had just finished an assignment and walked into the office, finding Jones on the computer as he usually was. He plopped down on the couch and intentionally let out a sigh, loud enough for Jones to hear.

"Something wrong?" Jones said.

"No, not really."

"Then what was the sigh for?"

"Oh, nothing I guess," Recker said.

"I think I know you better than that. What are you not happy with? Did you not like the conclusion of your spousal abuse case?"

"No, it turned out fine. I did like you asked and just roughed him up some."

"You preferred taking him out permanently?"

"Well after his ribs heal, there's a good chance we'll wind up dealing with him again. You know I don't like to handle the same people more than once."

"Well, it's all in the interest of trying to keep a lower profile," Jones said. "We're trying to prevent what happened at the end of our last stop, remember?"

"Yeah, I understand your reasons for it, but it doesn't mean I have to like it. It also doesn't mean it's going to change anything. Might not kill anybody for the next year and we could still wind up in the same boat."

"Yes, I'm aware. But can we just try it my way for a little longer before you break out your artillery?"

"I guess," Recker said, letting out another sigh to indicate his displeasure.

"What else is bothering you? Is it just the fact you haven't killed anybody in six months and you're getting an itchy trigger finger?"

"That's part of it."

"Is killing really so much ingrained into your soul you can't find another way to settle things?" Jones said.

"We seem to go over this every couple of months since we've known each other. It's not the killing per se, it's that sometimes it's the only way to handle things. Why postpone the inevitable?"

"Because I don't believe it is inevitable."

"That's the fundamental difference between us," Recker said. "You believe people can change and I don't."

"You just don't want to believe people can change."

"David, out of all the people I've killed since we started this, which one of those do you honestly believe would have never committed another crime if I had let them live?"

"Well...," Jones said, struggling to come up with a name.

"Exactly."

"Part of it is self-preservation. I'm trying to prevent another ending like the one in Philadelphia."

"All the planning in the world won't change that."

"Well I disagree."

"You know my philosophy. You're just as likely to run into trouble as you are to walk. You're just getting there faster. Historically, Detroit's been one of the most violent cities in the country with some of the highest murder rates. Sometimes you gotta fight fire with fire. If I bump a few criminals off, is it really going to put me on the radar?"

"So, if I give you the thumbs up to kill the next ten people you come across, will it make you happier?"

"Eh," Recker said with a shrug of the shoulder.

Jones threw his hands up in frustration. "What is it you're looking for then?"

"I dunno."

Jones could see in Recker's mannerisms and body language, he was troubled by something. It couldn't have just been his unhappiness about the way they were now working. There must have been something else on his mind. After a few minutes of silence, Jones thought he might have come up with a solution. Recker hadn't spoken of Mia in about three months. Jones figured his friend might have been missing her.

"Is it Mia?"

"What?" Recker said.

"When was the last time you spoke with her?"

"A few months I guess."

"Is that why you're unhappy?"

"I didn't say I was unhappy."

"You didn't have to. It's written on your face," Jones said.

"Oh."

"So?"

In prior years, Recker might not have been so forthcoming and honest in his answers. But with the relationship and rapport he and Jones had built up, they no longer seemed to keep things to themselves anymore. They were even becoming comfortable in talking about their unpleasant thoughts they used to keep private. Recker briefly thought about not talking about it any further but eventually relented and came clean.

"I dunno. It's a bunch of things I guess."

"Such as?" Jones said.

"Our work here, our life here, Mia, Philly... all of it."

"It's not just the killing thing bothering you, is it? You're just unhappy about being here in general."

Recker took a deep breath before answering. "Yeah," he said. "I thought with time I'd be better with this."

"Well six months isn't exactly a lot of time."

"I know. But it's just... I dunno, I guess I just felt like Philly was my home. I never really had one before. I felt at ease there, comfortable. Moved all over ever since I was eighteen. Sticking in one spot always felt like a dream to me. Something unattainable. I guess since I finally got a taste of what amounted to one, it's been hard to let go."

"I can understand. But maybe it's because you haven't really tried to fit in here," Jones said. "I've noticed you haven't done the same things you did there."

"Trying to do what you suggested and keep a lower profile. Fewer contacts and people who know me."

"You know we can't go back, right?"

Recker didn't reply and just shrugged his shoulders.

"Mike, if we ever go back there, the CIA will latch onto you again in a heartbeat. You somehow dodged a bullet the last time. But you're not Houdini. The next time you most likely won't be so lucky."

"Maybe so."

"Is it because you miss Mia?"

"Well, I do miss her. But as far as I know she's still with whats-his-name."

"Josh."

"Yeah."

"So why haven't you established contacts here like you did in Philadelphia?"

"To try and avoid the personal entanglements," Recker said.

"Well I can understand such an approach in terms of pretty female friends, but what about people like Tyrell, Vincent, Jeremiah? You haven't met any of those types here."

"I don't know. Just didn't care as much this time I guess."

"I wonder how Tyrell is," Jones said. "He grew on me."

"I talked to him about a month ago. He said he's doing all right."

"Did you tell him where we were?"

"No. He asked, and he wondered when we'd be back, but I didn't say."

As Recker sat there, Jones could tell his mind started drifting away to other things. The professor kept talking but Recker wasn't responding. It was clear to him Recker wasn't ignoring him, as the blank stare on his face was an indication his thoughts were elsewhere.

"Mike? What is it?"

Recker snapped out of his stare and looked over at his partner without saying a word. He just looked at him for a few moments as if he was still thinking.

"You said we couldn't go back to Philly because of the CIA," Recker said.

"Yes?"

"What if we could?"

"I'm sure there's a point in there somewhere though I can't seem to find it."

"If we could be assured the CIA isn't on my trail anymore, would you consider going back?"

"I suppose, theoretically, I would think about it," Jones said. "I don't know how you would go about getting such an assurance though."

"Only way I know of is to ask."

"Now you're just talking crazy."

"Lawson. If I could talk to her again, I could find out."

"And how do you propose on doing that?"

"If I can get a message to her, I can find out whether I'm still in the CIA crosshairs."

"Seems risky," Jones said.

"I think I can trust her. She easily could've killed me before."

"What makes you think she wouldn't try it the second time?"

"Faith."

"Faith? Since when was faith a word you employed?" Jones said.

"Gotta start sometime, right?"

"I'm not sure I'm on board with this plan of yours. We've successfully gotten away from the CIA, away from the police pressure in Philadelphia, we've started over, and you want to ignore it all and go back to it. There's just no logic to it."

"I never said I was logical."

Knowing he wasn't likely to talk his friend out of whatever was floating around inside his mind, Jones threw his hands up in defeat. "Do as you wish. I know you're probably not going to change your mind."

"I don't think it'll hurt just to have a conversation with her," Recker said.

"And like I said, I think you're just talking crazy."

2

It'd been a couple days since Recker had talked about reconnecting with Michelle Lawson and Jones had hoped he'd given up on the idea. The professor was mistaken, though, and disappointed when one morning Recker came into the office looking for one of his burner phones. Recker rifled through one of the desk drawers until he pulled one out.

"This one good?" Recker asked.

"They're all good, Michael."

"Well, not traceable, right?"

Jones stopped typing and looked at his partner with a strange face, not believing he actually asked the question. "Do you really believe I would have a traceable phone?"

"I'm just making sure."

"Can I ask what you're planning on doing with it?"

"I think you already know the answer," Recker said.

"That's what I was afraid of. You're really planning on calling her?"

"Why not? Don't you think it's worth knowing if they're going to keep on pursuing me or whether they've got other fish to fry? The worst she can say is I'm still on their radar."

"Assuming she's going to tell you the truth," Jones said.

"I think she will."

"And how do you plan on getting in touch with her? Do you have her number in your little black book?"

"Don't be ridiculous. You know I don't have a little black book. I'll find her the easiest way possible. I'll call up the agency and ask for her."

Recker immediately called the agency's main number, and while he knew it was unlikely he'd be connected to her right away, he left a message for her.

"Just tell her John Smith would like to speak with her. She'll know who I am."

Recker left a callback number and tossed the phone down on the desk.

"When do you think you'll hear back from her?" Jones said. "Assuming you do?"

"She'll call back. Even if it's just out of curiosity. I'd expect it to be pretty quick."

The call came even quicker than Recker expected. His phone rang about thirty minutes after leaving the message for Lawson. Recker and Jones looked at each other as they heard the ringer go off, neither expecting it to be quite so soon. Jones didn't appear to be pleased the call was being returned at all and began squirming in his seat as he anticipated the contents of the conversation. Recker walked over to the phone, and after the fourth ring, finally picked up.

"You're faster than I anticipated," Recker said. "I wasn't expecting you to call for a little while yet."

"Well, when a rogue super-agent who's missing for several years leaves me a message, I usually assume it's urgent," Lawson said.

"Fair enough. I was hoping to have another discussion with you."

"Seems like we are, doesn't it?"

"How about we do it in person? Phones have more ways of being traced than most people realize."

"Where and when?"

"How about tomorrow, say noon?"

"I think I can manage that. Where?"

"Are you still in New York?"

"Yes."

"There's a pizza joint on eighth called Anthony's. I'll be inside in one of the booths waiting for you," Recker said.

"Can't make it at a park or something?"

"Too public. I wouldn't want to meet another of those treacherous darts you used like last time in case I've misjudged you."

"I guess I could go for a slice, anyway."

"I'll see you then."

Recker put the phone down on the desk and kept his hand on it as he looked at the wall, deep in thought. Jones watched him for a few moments, waiting for him to reveal his plans in more detail. Though Jones overheard the parts of the conversation he most needed, he still assumed there was more to it. After several minutes ticked by, he tired of waiting,

"Are you going to share the gist of the conversation with me?"

"Weren't you listening?" Recker said.

"Yes, but all I got out of it was that you're meeting her in New York tomorrow at noon at a pizza place called Anthony's."

"That's all there was."

"How do you know this is a good spot to meet?"

"I've been there before. When I worked in Centurion, I visited the place a few times for business purposes. It's a busy place, people going in and out all the time. Plus, there's a back door."

"That doesn't really make it any better than meeting out in the open," Jones said. "All that means is that after your meeting is over, that there could be people waiting for you outside. It doesn't really change anything."

"You're right. But don't you think it'd be nice to know if I still have to look over my shoulder?"

"Yes, it would be. But I don't know if the risks outweigh the potential rewards."

"David, I just don't want to keep staying here, wondering if they're coming in another six months. I want to know. And if it means they take me for good this time... well, I guess it's better to just get it over with."

A peculiar look came over Jones' face, worried about his friend's mental condition. Considering Recker was the ultimate survivor, a fighter, someone who never quit, to hear him talk about getting it over with was somewhat alarming. Recker walked over to a computer and started figuring out his itinerary. It was over six hundred miles to go along with a nine-hour drive to head back to New York. It'd be the first time Recker set foot in New York since his time at Centurion ended. He thought back to a few of the meetings he'd previously had at Anthony's Pizza, where he gleaned information for an upcoming assignment from confidential sources. Though he knew Jones had a valid point about walking into trouble once he left the restaurant, it wasn't totally accurate. One of the reasons Recker picked Anthony's was because of his history there. Recker got to know the owner of the joint and knew that through the kitchen was a door leading to an upstairs office. From the office was a fire escape leading to the roof, and the businesses attached to it. He'd gotten in trouble there once before with some people who weren't what they appeared to be and had to use the route as an escape path. It was one of the reasons Recker befriended the owner, though he led him to believe he was an undercover FBI agent, since CIA operatives were not supposed to conduct operations within United States borders. It was always a good idea to make friends in places you might have to make a quick and unexpected exit out of.

"When do you plan to start this trek of yours?" Jones asked.

"Well, if I leave by one, then I should get there about ten or so. Should be enough time if I don't hit traffic."

"Do you not plan on sleeping?"

"I figured I'd knock off a little early tonight. If I go to bed around eight or nine, it'll give me three or four hours. That's enough," Recker said. "Think you can hold down the fort for a day until I get back?"

Jones faked a smile. "I'm sure I can manage."

The rest of their day went by without incident or any issues needing immediate attention. That enabled Recker to enact his plan by leaving the office at eight o'clock to get a few hours of sleep before his big meeting. Right on time, he woke up after a three-hour sleep and left at 1am. Jones didn't get much sleep either, spending most of the night tossing and turning as he worried whether Recker was making a mistake and walking into another trap. He probably wouldn't feel at ease until his partner texted or called to let him know the meeting was over, or what was more likely, when Recker was back in Michigan.

Recker arrived in New York a few minutes after ten and spent an hour driving around the city. Just being back there after such a long time away felt soothing to him. Until he made his way to Philadelphia, he'd always considered New York home, though for different reasons than how he considered Philly. It's where the Centurion offices were and he often stayed there between missions, at least before he met Carrie. Cruising around the streets, it almost felt like he'd never left. He remembered the street names, the buildings, the businesses scattered throughout the city, it actually seemed therapeutic for him. After reminiscing to his satisfaction for a while, Recker finally wound up at Anthony's at 11:30. One of his personal rules was to always be first at a meeting, just in case shenanigans were about to happen. Sometimes it couldn't be helped when he arrived at a conference later than whoever he was meeting, but when he was able to, he liked to scout around ahead of time. Walking into Anthony's, the place hadn't changed in the time he'd been gone. The tables, the counters, the menus, even the pictures on the wall. Everything was exactly the same as he remembered them. The place was starting to fill up, but Recker saw an open booth near the back of the establishment against the far wall. He'd no sooner sat down when he heard someone shout his name. Well, his former name anyway.

"John!" a man shouted.

Recker took a sharp look to his left and saw Anthony, the shop's owner, with a big smile on his face and walking toward his table. The two shook hands as Recker greeted his acquaintance, who sat down across from him.

"I was sure I'd never see you again," Anthony said, almost in disbelief now Smith was there again in his restaurant.

"It's been a long time."

"Yeah, it's been what, three, four years?"

"Yeah, about that."

"Well you're looking good. Where you been all this time?"

"I've been all over. Overseas, Philly, Michigan, spent some time in Ohio, they're running me ragged."

"What are you doing back in town? Here to stay?"

"Got a meeting here in a little bit. Figured I'd do it in the best pizza shop in town," Recker said, smiling.

"Hey, you know it. You want a slice and a Coke?"

"That's an offer I couldn't refuse."

"My man, I'll be right back."

A minute later, Anthony brought back two slices of pizza and a soda for his guest. The owner sat down so they could continue their conversation as his guest ate. Recker nodded his head, looking satisfied as he quickly downed the first piece of pizza.

"I've missed this," Recker said.

"How could you not miss the best pizza in town?" Anthony asked, laughing.

"You still have the office upstairs?"

"Yeah. Why? You gonna be needing it?"

"Ahh, you never know. I don't think so, but it's good to know it's there if the need arises."

"Some things never change, huh? I'll make sure the entrance by the kitchen's unlocked for you just in case."

"I appreciate it."

The two talked for a few more minutes before Anthony left, attending to other customers. The counter was starting to get busy. Recker finished his last remaining slice as he waited for his counterpart to arrive. He didn't have long to wait. He pulled out his phone to look at the time. It was 11:55. He took a quick look around the restaurant and saw a familiar face coming through the front doors. Lawson also liked to arrive ahead of schedule, just not as early as Recker. She stood near the counter as she looked around, not yet seeing Recker near the back. He took a deep sigh before revealing himself, just in case it was his last taste of freedom for a while. After a few more seconds, Recker stood up in front of his table in order for Lawson to see him. Once they locked eyes, she hesitated and looked away for a moment. She ordered a slice before walking over. Recker remained standing until she found her way to his table, not sitting down until she did as well. Lawson put a file folder down on the table as she nestled into the booth.

"Thanks for coming," Recker said.

"I haven't had a good piece of pizza in a while," she said, smiling. "So, what's this about?"

"A few things I guess. How'd you make out with the mess we left back in Philly?"

"Davenport's been fired and will never hold a government position again."

"And Agent 17?"

"It was wrapped up to everyone's satisfaction."

"And John Smith?"

"His case was closed since he's living a quiet life in Detroit."

Recker's mouth dropped open as he looked at her, surprised she knew where he was.

"Yes, we know where you are," Lawson said.

"How?"

"A good secret intelligence agency doesn't divulge their secrets."

Recker snickered as he took a sip of his soda.

"Is that what you're worried about?" Lawson asked.

"What makes you think I'm worried about anything?"

"Well I assume it's not because you decided to take me

up on my job offer. You wouldn't have requested this meeting if you were."

"You're smart."

"Thank you. It's nice to hear it sometimes."

"I guess I just wanted to know if I was still on the radar."

"Why? Figuring on blowing something up in Detroit?"

"Not yet. I guess I'm just getting tired of looking over my shoulder and wondering what's coming," Recker said.

"If you're in the tunnel and seeing the light of an oncoming train, it isn't gonna be us. You're clear. Your case is closed, you're not deemed a threat in any way to this agency or any other."

"Is that only when you're around?"

"No," Lawson said, opening up the folder. She removed some documents and slid them across the table for Recker to look at.

The papers consisted of memos and reports about Recker. It had different communications from Lawson, Director Roberts, as well as a few others talking about their findings in regard to Recker. They all seemed to agree their time and efforts were better spent elsewhere. He was no longer deemed a security risk, or a threat. Lawson assumed he would have trouble believing it just coming from her mouth and figured bringing some proof would help soothe his mind a little.

"You're free. You can go and do whatever you want without looking for us," Lawson said.

"Even back to Philly?"

"Even back to Philly. If we really wanted you, we

would've picked you back up again when you set foot in Detroit six months ago."

"Are you really not going to tell me how you managed to figure out where I was?"

Lawson looked around, then leaned forward before spilling her secret. "You probably should've gotten a new car after our last encounter."

Recker leaned back, with a peculiar look on his face, getting the hint. "No, I checked the car inside and out before I left."

"You probably should've checked the license plate."

"There's nothing on the license plate, I looked."

"You know the square little registration sticker in the corner? We replaced it with one which doubles as a GPS tracker," Lawson said.

Recker smiled, realizing she got one over on him. "I must be slowing down in my old age."

"We can be pretty clever sometimes. You know how it is. So, are you ever gonna tell me about the guy you're working with?"

"Who?" Recker asked, feigning ignorance.

"You know, the smaller guy you work with. Kind of looks like a nerd."

"I don't know who you're talking about."

Lawson smiled, impressed he was going the distance with his story, not that she really expected anything less. She probably would have been more surprised if he'd actually admitted he had a partner. Not one to give up herself, she opened her folder up again and pulled out some pictures and slid them across the table. Recker hesitantly picked up the 4x6 photos and went through them one at a time. He peered up over the pictures at Lawson, wondering how he could have been so sloppy. Every picture was one of him, or Jones, or of the both of them together since they moved to Detroit.

"So, what are you going to do with these?" Recker said.

"Nothing. I didn't bring them to blackmail you or warn you of anything. Just to let you know we're aware of your whereabouts. If we wanted you, we'd have picked you up already. I figured the pictures would be more proof for you to trust me. I recall you saying something to me about not trusting people. I figured it still applied."

"You can't put a name to the face?"

"No. We've run him through all the databases we have and we can't seem to come up with anything. Who is he?"

"Who's asking? Michelle Lawson the person? Or Michelle Lawson the CIA agent?"

"Does it make a difference?"

"Maybe."

"Let's say Michelle Lawson the person then."

Recker nodded, then looked away at the bustling crowd, trying to figure out how he'd phrase the answer. "His name is David. His situation is a little different from mine."

"David what?"

"Doesn't really matter. Neither name I'd give you is his real identity anyway and it wouldn't come up in your computers, regardless."

"So why him? What made you throw in with him?" Lawson said.

"He actually sought me out," Recker said, remembering their first meeting at the airport. "He gave me an interesting proposition, and I decided to take him up on it."

"Doing what? Playing hero?"

"He wanted to make a difference somewhere. Help good people who needed help. Plus, I needed a job and a reason to keep going after London."

"I'm guessing he's pretty good with computers."

"Yeah, you could say."

"He'd have to be to hide his identity even from us, not to mention get the information you guys need to do what you're doing," Lawson said. "So, is he on the run too?"

"Uh, not from you. Why all the interest in him? Wondering if he's a former agent too?"

"No. It's more of a personal curiosity. Just wondering how and why you got into what you're doing now. So, what makes you wanna go back to Philly?"

"I dunno. I guess I just felt a connection there. Like I belonged."

"Well, you won't hear from us again, unless you decide you want to join up again."

"Not likely."

"The police now know you there, though, so you'll have to deal with them on your own. But according to Commissioner Boyle, half the force wants to shake your hand, though the other half probably wants to shoot you on sight. But you know we can't do much about it. Your problem."

"I know," Recker said. "What about you? Eventually

they're gonna realize I'm back. Are they gonna give you a hard time about not taking me in?"

"Eh, not really my concern. I don't answer to them. If they ask, I'll just say you escaped."

"And if they ask for your help again?"

"We're not in that business anymore. We have other, more pressing matters to attend to."

Satisfied with her answers so far, Recker started turning the questions around. "So, what do they have you working on these days? Besides keeping tabs on me obviously. You hunting down a new rogue agent?"

"No, not at the moment. Right now, they have me on special assignment. For the past few months I've been helping to run Centurion since they're down a director. As soon as they appoint a new head, they'll switch me to something else."

"I hope you've eliminated the program where they terminate good agents for no apparent reason."

"Yeah, it's being run a little differently these days. Hopefully, for the better."

"If you're involved, I'm sure it is."

Recker was still fumbling with the pictures, periodically looking at them, but eventually stopped and attempted to slide them back over to his guest. Lawson, though, returned the favor and slid them back to him.

"You can keep them if you like," Lawson said. "I don't think we really have need for them anymore."

Recker smiled, appreciative of the gesture. "If you're not careful, I might actually end up liking you."

"Now that'd be a catastrophe."

"This little meeting of ours almost seems like it's going too well. You don't happen to have a few men waiting outside, ready to pump some lead into me, do you?"

"Now where would you get such a crazy idea?"

"It might've been mentioned to me somewhere along the drive here."

"Your partner thought it was a bad idea, huh?"

"Something like that," Recker said. "He's not as trusting as I am."

"Well you can take those pictures back to him and let him know neither of you have anything to fear from us. You don't have to look over your shoulder anymore."

3

———

Recker's meeting with Lawson took much longer than he had anticipated as they didn't wrap things up until two o'clock. They enjoyed talking to each other openly and honestly, without the need for secrecy as so often summed up meetings with people in their line of work. By the time they finished, Recker was convinced he had nothing to fear from her. He also knew he didn't have to worry about being shot once he left the restaurant, as Jones had suggested. When Recker did finally leave the restaurant, he drove around the city for another hour, soaking in the sights of The Big Apple before he returned to Michigan.

He got back to the Detroit area around midnight and immediately went to his apartment to catch up on some much-needed sleep. Before doing so, he let Jones know everything went OK at the meeting and he'd fill him in when he got to the office in the morning. Recker didn't provide any other details. He figured if he dropped the bombshell that the CIA still knew where they were, and had the pictures to prove it, neither of them would wind up sleeping. With the way Jones' mind worked, Recker knew he'd stay up all night peppering him with questions on how it was possible and trying to think of a way to get out from underneath their grasps.

Once Recker arrived in the office in the morning, he was armed with some breakfast sandwiches, along with the photos Lawson had given him. He figured it was about to be a long day. He just hoped Jones didn't freak out as much as he thought he would. After both sat down to start eating, Recker reached into his pocket to remove the pictures. He placed them face down in front of Jones.

"What's this?" Jones asked, putting the remaining half of his sandwich down.

"A gift from my meeting."

Jones wiped his hands and looked at his partner, sure he was not going to like what he was about to see as he picked them up. There were ten pictures in all, and with each one he passed, Jones' face became even more flabbergasted. He didn't glance up at Recker one time as he perused the pictures. Recker was trying to analyze his friend's face as he looked through the photos and could obviously see Jones had become uncomfortable with what he was seeing, though he didn't voice any concerns yet. Maybe he was just too surprised for him to vocalize anything. After looking through the set of pictures three times, Jones finally was able to take his eyes off them as he set them back down on the table.

"These were from Ms. Lawson?"

"Yep," Recker said.

"She knows where we are. She knows who I am."

"Well, not quite. They now know you're involved and have a picture of you. Fortunately for you, your face isn't recognized in any of their databases. They haven't actually put a name to you yet."

"I guess that's something," Jones said, only looking slightly relieved. "So, what does all this mean? Should we be reinforcing the doors today?"

Recker let out a small laugh. "No. We're in the clear. They're not coming for us, or more specifically, me. They've known where we were since the day we got here. If they wanted us, they would've gotten us long before now."

"So, what now then? What are their plans?"

"They have none. Lawson said I've been taken off their to-do-list. I don't have to look over my shoulder anymore. No one's coming."

Jones looked at him incredulously with the revelation. "Are you sure you can believe her?"

"Well, she's had the chance to take me out twice. There's no logical reason to let me walk away twice."

"I see," Jones said, seemingly having a hard time processing everything. "And uh... what of me? Am I included in that?"

"They're not after you. She wondered who you were more out of a personal curiosity than professional interest. She gave me those pictures so I'd believe that they weren't after us. It's proof that they could've taken us out at any time since we've been here. They know this office and where we are at this exact minute. They don't care."

"Startling."

"The man who originally put the kill order on me is no longer in control of Centurion," Recker said.

"This is... a lot to take in right now."

"I know. But it's also grounds for us to go back to Philly, right? Admit it, you don't like it here as much as back there, do you?"

"I will admit a certain fondness for there that I have not yet acquired here. But that may also be that I don't get out as much here, with having the bedroom off the main office," Jones said.

"We established something there. A name, an identity, an intimidation factor... we haven't gotten that here. And maybe in time we will, but we already invested ourselves there."

"And the police? Did Ms. Lawson give you assurances about them as well?"

"No, of course not. The police are our concern. But that's the way it's gonna be no matter where we go. We can handle them, though. Besides, Lawson told me half the police force there is on our side, anyway."

Jones took another bite of his sandwich before leaning back in his chair, arms crossed, giving the matter more thought. He wasn't against the move back to Philadelphia, and he'd probably enjoy it more than he'd let on, but part of him felt that by moving again so soon, they just wasted the last six months. But he did miss the city streets, the vibe of the place, the few relationships he did have, such as Mia, and even the few times he'd met or talked with Tyrell. He still owned the office and laundromat, so it'd be easier moving back there than it was setting up shop in Detroit. Recker had moved to another computer to work on things, giving Jones some time to himself to collect his thoughts on the subject. After thirty minutes, Jones was ready to announce his opinion.

"If I do agree to go back, we cannot just pick up and leave. We have a few things to finish here, people who need help. I don't want to just abandon them."

"Agreed," Recker said.

"But I can start the process by unplugging the software program, so to speak, so we don't get additional cases."

"How many do we have now?"

"Four. I would think as soon as they're done, we can head back."

They talked a little while longer about the ramifications of moving back, with Recker wanting to make sure Jones was completely on board and not just giving him lip service. The longer they discussed it, the more comfortable Jones became with it, and sounded just as excited as Recker was to be about going back. He did miss it too; he was just more convincing with putting up a front to disguise it. Recker immediately started working on their remaining cases, wanting to wrap things up as quickly as possible. He hoped to be back in Philadelphia within a week, which was probably a bit of a reach.

Once Recker latched onto an idea and really got behind something, it would be wise for everyone to get out of his way. Though Jones had doubts he'd be able to finish the four cases within a week, Recker worked over-time and sacrificed a few hours of sleep every night in order to accomplish it. Eight days after they agreed to return to Philadelphia, they wrapped up all their remaining cases in Detroit. Except for one last hiccup. Jones had a moving van outside the office and most of their things had already been removed from the office. But he left one computer running until the very last minute, just in case of an emergency. He had a fear how the moment they left, something major would go down and somebody would get hurt or killed. Something which could've been prevented if they were still around. Jones was standing by the computer, getting ready to shut it off and pull the plug, when he got one final alert. It was a familiar name and phone number. Recker just finished putting the last of the boxes in the van when he walked into the office and saw Jones standing in front of the computer.

"What's up?" Recker asked.

Jones turned to him without saying a word. His face did all the talking Recker needed though.

"Don't even tell me," Recker said. "David, we're ready to go."

Jones didn't reply and turned back to the computer, looking at the screen. Recker, slightly agitated Jones was considering another case when they were just about to leave, walked over to him. His first inclination was to not look at anything and turn everything off for Jones, then they wouldn't have to bother with anything. But, like Jones, Recker couldn't just turn his back on someone who legitimately needed help. After all, it was what he did, what he lived for. Reluctantly, Recker stood beside his partner and looked at the screen. After quickly scanning the monitor, Recker looked a little more closely at the information. His face turned from annoyed to concern, then to anger. He had a feeling this would happen. Some people just couldn't change their spots. The two men stood there silently, both knowing what was about to happen. Jones looked over at Recker, and sighed, feeling like this might've been his fault. If he'd have let Recker do what he wanted to do in the first place, Teresa Golden might not have been suffering from the new batch of bruises at the hands of her husband. Jones picked up another text message sent from Teresa to her sister, detailing the latest attack. Though her sister implored her to go to the authorities, and the hospital, Teresa refused both requests, not wanting to get anyone else involved. Richard Golden blamed his wife for him getting beat up, believing she must have gabbed about his infractions to somebody.

"I guess he didn't get the message," Recker said.

"I should've let you do what you wanted from the start."

"You can't blame yourself for other people's actions."

"But you predicted this would happen. I should've listened," Jones said.

"Yeah, but you can't take responsibility for it. It's on them. Not on you."

"Should we take care of this before we go?"

Recker reached inside his coat and removed a gun,

double checking to make sure it was loaded. "Absolutely. But we'll take care of it my way."

"Understood."

"Why don't you finish up here and start heading back? I'll do what I have to do then meet up with you somewhere along the road."

Recker immediately left the office and got in his truck to meet Golden before he got to work. Recker wasn't going to be able to catch him before he left his house and he wasn't sure if his wife and kids would still be there, anyway. And Recker wasn't going to do what he had to in front of them. Golden worked in downtown Detroit at an office building with a parking garage. Recker would be there waiting for him. From their initial investigation of Golden, before Recker dusted him up inside his home, they knew Golden got to work at nine o'clock every day. Recker got to the garage at 8:30. He parked near the entrance inside so once he saw Golden arrive, he could follow him to his spot. At 8:55, Recker spotted Golden's car enter the garage. He gave Golden a short lead of a few seconds before tailing him. Once Golden pulled into a spot against the wall, Recker pulled up behind the rear bumper of the car, blocking it from reversing. Golden was consumed with getting some of his things together and didn't even noticed the impending danger looming. Recker noticed there were no security cameras near the entrance, so he didn't have to worry about being spotted. It wouldn't have concerned him if there were since he was leaving the city right after this, anyway.

Recker got out of his car and walked around the hood

until he stood just outside of the driver's side window. Golden was leaning over toward the passenger side seat where he was looking through some papers, still oblivious to the dangerous man who was only inches away on the other side of the glass. Recker figured he'd make a grand entrance and took the handle of his gun and smashed the window. Golden jumped in his seat, surprised at the falling glass. He put his arms up over his head to try to protect himself. Once he put his arms down and looked at the man on the other side of his window, he started to shake. It was partly out of fear, knowing what his attacker was capable of, remembering what he did to him before. The other half of him was shaking because he was injured, as small pieces of glass lodged into his face and arm. Recker turned the gun around and pointed it at the frightened man.

"Guess you didn't get the message from our last meeting," Recker said.

"Go to hell. What I do with my family is my business."

"Wrong answer."

Recker didn't wish to continue the conversation any longer or put off the inevitable. He simply pulled the trigger and fired two rounds into Golden's chest. Recker's victim slumped over across the middle console, perishing immediately upon the bullets entering his body. Recker stood there for a moment, analyzing his work, and shook his head.

"Some people just don't get it," Recker whispered. "Give them all the chances in the world and they just don't get it."

Recker then put his gun away and went back to his car. He peeled out of the garage and made his way to the highway to trek back to Philadelphia. He sent a text message to Jones to let him know his work was done and how he'd meet him back in the office when they arrived back in town. With Jones getting a head start on him, he was already moving some of the boxes into the office by the time Recker got there nine hours later. Jones didn't bother asking him any questions about how things turned out with Golden. He knew what had been done. They finished unpacking and moving all their equipment back into the office, getting finished around midnight. Considering neither had bothered to get a new apartment yet, they each wound up taking separate couches to sleep for the night.

When they awoke in the morning, Jones wasted no time in getting his computers up and running. He had hooked everything up the night before, but running his programs and getting them to coordinate the way he wanted, took some time. As he did it, Recker restocked his gun cabinet with the weapons he'd just stashed in the corner before going to bed.

"How long you gonna take?" Recker asked.

"Not too much longer. Everything should be ready to go in an hour or so," Jones said. "It will take a little longer until we start getting cases again. The program will have to start over again and go through mountains of data before it starts spitting things out."

"Oh."

"Itching to get back to work already?"

"Just wondering what I'll do until then."

"Why don't you get out, see the city. I'll let you know when it's time."

"Maybe I will."

"Maybe let Mia and Tyrell know we've returned. Maybe look for a new apartment."

"That reminds me, what are you gonna do for a new place?" Recker asked.

"I hadn't really given it much thought. The place in Detroit seemed to work well, so I thought I may just stay here."

"But there's no extra room here."

"No, but I don't really need much," Jones said. "I can sleep on the couch. We've got a bathroom, a TV, I don't really require much else. Besides, there's nobody else coming in here except you and me so I don't have to worry about any unwelcome visitors."

"You want me to just stay here too?"

"No, of course not. Don't be foolish. Go get a new place, enjoy your apparent newfound freedom. You don't appear to have to hide from the CIA any longer, so you shouldn't stay cooped up in here. But don't forget, one of us is still a government fugitive, so staying in here will be fine for me. I have no complaints," Jones said, forging a smile.

"OK, well, let me know when everything's ready."

"You'll be the first to know."

Recker thought about his living arrangements and figured his last apartment worked fine for him. It was in a nice area and relatively close to everything. When he went back to see if anything was still available, his old apartment had been rented out, but there was another unit almost identical to his, the difference being this one had a small balcony off the living room. When he left for Detroit, he left most of his furniture behind. The only thing he took with him was the TV. He signed the papers for the apartment, but the unit wouldn't be ready until the following day, which gave him some time to order some furniture so he wouldn't be sitting on the floor for too long.

With his living situation taken care of, Recker started driving around the city again. Though he wasn't going anywhere in particular, and didn't have a specific destination in mind, he somehow found himself at the hospital where Mia worked. Outside of Jones, she was his closest friend, so maybe it was just instinctual when he wound up there. Once he parked, Recker sat in his car for a few minutes, wondering if he really wanted to go in. Not that he didn't want to see her, but it had been three months since they'd talked. He wasn't sure what type of reception he'd get. He never wound up telling Mia where he was going and she was the last one to try to communicate. She left a text message along with a voicemail Recker just never bothered returning. He wanted to, but something kept nagging at him to just let her go. For her own sake. He figured if he was gone, unlikely to ever return, she'd have been better off putting him out of her memory. And she couldn't if they continued talking. Part of him wondered if he would be better off driving away, not even telling her he was back. But he knew, somehow, someway, she'd find out he'd returned, and it'd probably be worse if she found out than if he told her himself.

After ten more minutes, and a lot of thought and reflection, Recker decided to go in. He asked at the front desk whether Mia was working, and once it was confirmed, he went over to the cafeteria, their usual meeting spot. Though he didn't know her exact schedule, going from memory, when she worked day shift, he figured he had an hour or two to wait until she came down for lunch. It gave him more time to reflect on their relationship. It was additional time to think he really didn't need as he was already beating himself up over how he handled things with her. He sat at the back table and fiddled around with his fingers as he stared at his hands, wondering what he was going to say to her when he saw her. This was probably the most nervous he'd ever been.

And he was right. It was a long wait. Two hours that felt like it was two days. Mia walked into the cafeteria and got some food, not initially seeing her visitor. She didn't see him until she was looking for a seat in the crowded room. Recker was still fumbling with his hands and looking down at the table and never even saw her come in. When Mia's eyes finally did locate him, she couldn't believe what she was seeing at first. She looked away, hoping it was just a vision that would somehow go away. Maybe she'd been working too hard. It was no vision, though, no mind trick. She locked eyes on him once again, and instead of being happy he was there, anger started flowing through her veins. For the last three months, she tried to get him out of her system. Without hearing a word from him, she could only assume the worst, he was dead. On the nights when she convinced herself he was still alive, she could only assume he just didn't want anything to do with her anymore.

As she stood there, holding her tray, she struggled with whether she wanted to go sit with him and see what he wanted. She debated whether she'd be better off sitting by herself and pretending he wasn't even there. He didn't appear to be paying much attention anyway, she could quickly eat and be gone before he knew she was there. But she quickly dismissed the idea since Recker knew where she lived. He could always show up at her door. Or he could just come back another day. Even if she wanted to avoid him, she knew she couldn't do it for long. She eventually figured it would be better to see what he was doing there and walked over to his table. Recker was so fixated on his hands and his own thoughts he never even noticed someone standing across from him. It wasn't until Mia forcefully slammed her tray down on the table that he took his eyes off his hands. He looked up at her, licked his lips to remove the dryness, and gave a nervous-looking smile.

"What are you doing here?" Mia asked, still standing.

"You uh, gonna sit and eat?"

"I don't know if I'm gonna be here long enough."

Recker put his hand out, imploring her to sit. "Please."

Mia let out a sigh, thinking she shouldn't comply with his request, but reluctantly agreed and sat at the table.

"Thank you," Recker said.

Mia wasn't feeling too hospitable though. "So, what is

it you want?" she asked bluntly, devoid of almost any feeling.

"David and I are back in town."

"For good?"

"Yeah. Umm, I had another encounter with the CIA last week and they informed me I'm clear now. They're not looking for me anymore."

"Oh. So, what does that mean exactly?" Mia asked, several months of anger showing in her voice. "You just come back here six months after you left like nothing happened?"

"I know I didn't um..."

"Mike, I haven't heard from you in three months. I didn't know where you were, I didn't know what happened to you, I didn't even know if you were alive or dead."

"I know. I'm sorry."

"For the last three months, not one word from you. I just assumed you were dead. And now, suddenly, out of the blue, you're sitting here at my work for some reason."

"You have every right to be angry."

"You're damn right I'm angry. How else would you expect me to feel?"

Recker shrugged. "Nothing else."

"So why are you here? Just to say you're back? Injured? Have a gunshot wound you need me to look at?"

"No. I guess I deserve that though. To be honest, I really don't know what I'm doing here. I was just out driving around and suddenly I found myself here."

"When'd you get back?"

"Late last night."

"So where were you all this time?"

"We went to Detroit."

"Why? What was there?"

"People who needed help."

"I just don't understand what you want from me. You tell me you're leaving, you show up at my door shot again, then you're gone. You leave for six months, I don't hear from you for the last three of them then you just appear and say you're back."

"I dunno. I guess I just came here to say hi," Recker said, struggling to find something that would soothe her. "I missed you."

"You missed me?"

"Yeah. I don't know what else you want me to say."

"You know, there was a time when you could've said anything to me and I would've believed it," Mia said. "I would've followed you anywhere, done anything. But not now. Not anymore."

Recker nodded his head, feeling a sense of sadness, realizing he may have made a mistake in coming. "Are you still with uh, whatshisname?"

"Josh. And yes, we're still together," Mia said, a little perturbed that he still wouldn't say her boyfriend's name.

"Happy? He treating you well and all?"

"Yeah, basically. Sorry, there's nothing for you to beat him up over or kill him or anything."

Recker forced a smile, not taking offense at her harsh words, realizing her feelings had been hurt.

"Are you going to try and explain why you basically ignored me for the last three months?"

"I would but I don't know if anything I say will be good enough to satisfy you. Or satisfy me either."

"You can try."

"The only thing I can really say is I thought you'd be better off without me in your life. I wasn't sure if I was ever coming back. You found someone new, it seemed like you were moving on," Recker said. "I thought by continuing to talk to me, you would still be living in the past, instead of the future."

"And what do you think coming here now is doing?" Mia asked, still not cooling off.

Recker could see, no matter what he said, it wasn't going to make a difference. She had her mind made up. She was going to be angry, and there was no changing that. But he still couldn't blame her for it. She'd had three months to build up to this point. Three long months of hostility and she wasn't letting up. Right then, he figured maybe the best thing he could do was leave. He could see he wasn't doing anybody any good by being there.

"Well, I guess I've taken up enough of your time. Enjoy the rest of your lunch," Recker said.

"I still don't understand what it is you really want. You pull me in, then push me away, draw me close, then say we can't be together, then we kiss, then you leave, then you want to be friends, then you move away, then we're friends, then we don't talk, then you show up. You constantly tell me one thing, then do another. Over and over again."

"I guess I can't really dispute it, can I?"

"You could. You'd be wrong if you tried though. You just confuse me and I can't take it anymore. I won't. I deserve better."

"You're right. You do deserve better," Recker said, standing up.

"Leaving again? It seems it's what you do best. Push people away, run off, leave people behind. You only get involved with anybody if it suits whatever angle you're working at the time."

Recker still didn't take offense to anything she said. He seemed like a defeated man. Quite unlike himself. "I've never worked an angle with you. You take care of yourself."

He started to walk away but was stopped by Mia, who grabbed his forearm. She looked up at him, not wanting to end their conversation by being mad at each other, even if she was really the only one who seemed indignant.

"Mike, eventually you have to figure out what it is you really want. You have to admit to yourself that it's OK to let go of whatever it is that holds you back. But until you do, you'll never be at peace with yourself."

Recker gave her one last smile before walking away, thinking it might be the last time he ever saw her. He would have hoped their last meeting would be a more pleasant one, but he knew she had every right to bitch him out the way she did. Mia turned around to catch a final glimpse of him before he left, seeing him just in time to exit the cafeteria. She turned back toward her food and used her fork to play around with it, still steaming from their conversation. She shook her head, a flood of emotions overtaking her.

Recker left the hospital and had returned to his truck. He sat there for a few minutes, reflecting on his conversation with Mia. After getting her out of his mind, his phone rang just as he turned on the engine.

"I hope you have someone for me to shoot," Recker said, indicating his mood.

"Uh, no," Jones said. "But I did want to let you know everything is up and running."

"Great. Let me know when you have something. Preferably dangerous. And with people armed. The more dangerous the better."

Jones didn't quite know how to respond. "Umm, are you encountering some problems out there?"

"No, why would you think that?"

"Oh, no reason. What have you been doing?"

"I dunno. Just thought I'd try and fix a mistake."

"What kind of mistake?"

"It's nothing."

"I guess it didn't go so well."

"No, it didn't."

"Well, the good thing about mistakes is they can sometimes be erased," Jones said, offering some hope.

"Yeah, I don't know about this one. I think this might be one mistake that can't be fixed."

4

"Nice to see you return in one piece," Jones said.

"Huh?" Recker said.

Recker had just gotten back to the office after his outing at the hospital and he wasn't sure if he'd missed something. Maybe he was in a battle he wasn't aware of. He noticed Jones had set the Keurig up and went over to the counter to get a cup of coffee.

"Well there's no holes in me," Recker said, patting his chest and legs. "Did you have doubts about me coming back in one piece?"

"Well, after our conversation earlier, it sounded as if you'd just escaped from a confrontation."

"I did. Not of the physical variety though. Still, it was lethal nonetheless."

"Am I to assume you had a little chat with Mia?" Jones asked.

"Chat's not quite the word for it. Chat indicates a level

of respect and calmness between the two parties. There wasn't much of that going on."

"I take it she wasn't pleased to see you."

"No, not at all. It was more like she chewed me up, spit me out, then stomped on whatever was on the ground."

"You certainly are a glutton for punishment," Jones said. "Our first day back and you're already the worse for wear."

"I don't know what I was doing there. Trying to make things right I guess."

"You really do know how to put your foot in it, don't you? Well you can't say you don't deserve whatever tongue lashing she dished out. You've put Mia through the ringer."

Recker sighed, not wanting to hear about his shortcomings all over again. "Listen David, getting verbally ripped apart once a day is enough, OK? I don't really need it coming from you too."

"You're right. I'm sorry, I wasn't trying to pile it on."

"I know. Let's just not talk about Mia, OK?"

"As you wish."

"Anything on the horizon yet?" Recker asked, hoping for a case to take his mind off things.

"Sadly, no. Don't you have something else to keep you busy?"

"Well, I already got my apartment back. Well, not back. Different unit, same building."

"I guess everything's not so glum then."

"Easy for you to say. Maybe I'll check with Tyrell to see if anything's been brewing while we've been gone."

"Excellent idea."

Jones mostly just wanted to get Recker out of the office. Since they didn't have any cases at the moment, he worried in case Mia's verbal assault would have an adverse effect on Recker. Jones knew whenever Recker had personal problems, which wasn't often since they didn't have many friends, and they usually revolved around Mia, he usually stewed over it for most of the day. Jones didn't really want to play psychiatrist the first day they were back in town, no matter how much he cared for the both of them. He just had too much to do to get the systems back up and running properly.

While Recker was bothered by the events at the hospital, he didn't think she was wrong, and he didn't want to dwell on it either. Her feelings were what they were, and he wasn't going to be able to change it. The best thing he figured he could do was to get a beat on what was happening around town. Tyrell was usually the best person to get that information out of, so Recker pulled out his phone and gave him a call.

"Tyrell, what's going on?"

"Not much, man, how you doin'?"

"Good. I just wanted to let you know I was back in town."

"Really? We'll have to get together. You back for good or just to visit?"

"For good."

"Sweet, man, we can use you around here," Tyrell said.

"Why? Something wrong?"

"Ahh, you know, just the usual."

"That's one of the reasons I called. I just wanted to see what was happening out there and if there was anything I should know about."

"What, you mean like Vincent and Jeremiah going to war with each other? Stuff like that?"

"Yeah, that would qualify."

"Then nah, nothing big. Not yet, anyway."

"Do me a favor," Recker said. "Can you start spreading the word? I'm back in town."

"Why? You don't wanna make a grand entrance somewhere?"

"Not this time."

"Yeah, I can do that."

"Thanks. So, what's the word been since I've been gone? People been breathing easier?"

"Yeah, you ain't kidding. Lot of people not as worried about doing things because they knew they didn't have to deal with you once word got out you were gone."

"It's why I want word to get out that I'm back. Time to put a healthy dose of fear back into people," Recker said.

"I'll tell you what though, for as much damage as you inflict, I think the city missed you."

"Is that so?"

"Yeah. Like I said, you put fear into the underhanded folks, and the regular people, they feel like they got a guardian angel watching over their backs if someone starts messing with them."

"Well I don't know about the angel part."

"Plus, I think you help keep the peace, especially between men like Vincent and Jeremiah. They were too afraid to make a move on anyone out of fear you'd show up on the other side of them," Tyrell said. "Nobody wants to go up against you and make you an enemy. You know Vincent and Jeremiah are gonna wonder and worry why you're back, right? They're gonna worry the other brought you back to help them take the other out. They might wanna have a word."

"No, I'm not doing that again. I did it once before when I first got here. I'm not explaining myself or my intentions again. If they ask, tell them I haven't changed."

After his call with Tyrell concluded, Recker left the office and drove around for a while to pass the time. He didn't get back to the office until later in the day, bringing dinner back for him and Jones. The professor was armed with some information he might find useful, though not quite what Recker was hoping for.

"Figured you could use some food," Recker said, placing a sandwich and fries on the desk.

"Yes, I could. You know, I found out some interesting information while you were gone."

"We got a case?"

"No, but it's still interesting, anyway."

"I'd still prefer a case."

"I know, but listen to this," Jones said, looking at his computer screen after taking a bite of his sandwich. "I started digging into the crime statistics in the time we were away."

"You're right, it is interesting," Recker said, not really interested at all.

"No, since we've been gone, crime's gone up across the board."

"So?"

"So, it proves what we were doing before was effective. You were a deterrent."

"I'd rather have a case."

"Yes, I know. But that should make you feel good."

"I'll feel good when I have a case."

"It's coming," Jones said, getting more exasperated.

"If crime's up across the board, how come we don't have anything yet?"

"Mike, we just got here. Give it some time."

"Yeah, yeah. So, everything's been up since we've been gone?"

"Surprising to say, but yes. Small crimes up, major crimes up, violent crimes up, murders up."

"I think it's a little premature to say we were the difference," Recker said.

"Perhaps so. But the numbers are the numbers. I'm especially surprised by the murders being up."

"So, what's that say to you?"

"Maybe by you killing people, it prevented others from doing the same."

"And if that's the case, then maybe it throws a wrench into your idea of me handling things a different way."

"Possibly. But you know the saying, violence begets violence."

"I don't care what anybody says, being intimidating and violent will scare some people. The people who are violent and ruthless will still be, no matter what. I'm just taking them out of the equation."

"I don't suppose you'd be interested in handling things the way we did in Detroit, would you?" Jones asked.

"I'll handle things the way I think they need to be. No more, no less. If a gun's required, I'll use it. If it's not, I won't. I'm not going out of my way like I've done the last six months. It really didn't get us anywhere. Ask Teresa Golden."

"Mike, she was one example out of hundreds."

"That we know of. How do you know how many others are going to happen in the next few weeks or months?"

It was a familiar discussion between the two of them, one they seemed to have every few months, or after something extreme happened. It was likely to be a thorn of contention between them for as long as they would work together. Jones always advocated for handling things as diplomatically as possible with the least amount of violence. Recker usually opted for whatever would get the job done, as long as he wouldn't have to come back to the same situation at a later time. No matter how many times they discussed it, though, they both knew they weren't changing the other one's mind on it. They were both locked in to their positions and Recker didn't really care to talk about it anymore and changed the subject.

"You think you could still monitor the CIA like you did before?" Recker asked.

"For what purpose?"

"For the purpose of being safe and not taking chances."

"If you said you're not on the list anymore, I don't see what the point would be," Jones said.

"Like I said, just as a precaution. I believe Lawson at her word when she says I'm off the radar. But what if someone new comes along and decides to open my case up again for some reason?"

Jones nodded, seeing his position. "It will take a couple days but I can get the same program as before running."

"Even if nothing ever comes of it, I'd rather know what's coming instead of getting a surprise party."

It wasn't until the following day Jones found their first case to work on since they'd been back. Recker was at his new apartment getting the furniture delivery he'd ordered the previous day. He actually furnished it like a normal person this time instead of the bare bones approach he used before. He bought a sofa, recliner, dining room set, a bed, along with some tables. It was a new style for him, but he figured if they were making it home, maybe he should dress it up a little. Jones told him not to bother coming back to the office until he had something for him to work on since there was no reason for both of them to be there with nothing to do. As soon as Jones called, Recker left his swanky new place to head back to the office.

"So, what do we got?" Recker said, asking the moment he set foot in the office.

"We've got what may pass for our most difficult case yet."

"What? We've handled some tough stuff before."

"Yes, but none of those situations involved police officers," Jones said.

"Police?"

"Yes. It looks like our subject is one of Philadelphia's finest."

"Well that is a new one. What's the story?"

"The story is, apparently Officer Eduardo Perez has found himself on the hit list of a dangerous man," Jones said.

"How's that?"

"It seems that several years ago Officer Perez was responsible for arresting a man named Adrian Bernal. Mr. Bernal just got out of prison about a month ago and is already plotting his revenge."

"I take it Bernal is not someone to be taken lightly?"

"Very violent past and criminal record."

"I assume the police and Perez aren't aware he's coming?" Recker asked.

"No. He's made no apparent threats."

"Then how'd you pick up on it?"

"Because Mr. Bernal sent a text message to his girlfriend saying he was, 'going to get the stinking cop' who arrested him."

"Could be just talk," Recker said. "Criminals make threats all the time. They very rarely act on them. Especially on a cop."

"Well, it will be our job to ascertain the severity of the threat. That is, assuming you want to look into this."

"Why wouldn't we?"

"As I mentioned before, we've never had a police officer as someone who needed our protection. Things could get... hairy, as some would say."

"I don't think it really makes a difference, do you?"

"Well now that you're as known as you are, interacting with the police on any level is more dangerous than it's ever been. If this came up two years ago, it wouldn't be much of an issue since they had no idea who you were. Now they know your face. If you happen to come into contact with Officer Perez, even in the interest of helping him, and he recognizes you, he may arrest you before you can help him."

"Doesn't matter. The police aren't our enemy. We're on the same side."

"I agree," Jones said.

"We may have different methods, but we both want the same thing. To clean up the streets. They just have more rules than I do."

"It doesn't change the fact that you must tread carefully."

"I will. But we can't pass on this one. Even if it puts me on the hot seat. We can't sit still for someone killing a cop. Does Perez seem like he's on the up and up?"

"In what way? Like he's not dirty or something?" Jones asked.

"Yeah."

"From what I can gather, nothing seems out of the

ordinary. No complaints on file. He appears to be a good cop trying to do a good job."

"Then he is good enough for our help. There's too many police officers in this country getting ambushed or killed when all they're doing is trying to do the job they were hired for," Recker said. "You agree?"

"I've already said as much. As long as it doesn't end up with you in the back of a squad car."

"What district's Perez in?"

"He's assigned to the twenty-sixth," Jones said.

"Any idea how or when Bernal's going to enact this plan of his?"

"Not as of yet. I've still got some more digging to do though. I didn't want to get knee deep in research only for you to say to let the police handle it on their own."

"You know as well as I do I wouldn't have."

"Perhaps not."

"So how long's it gonna take you to get into the rest of it?" Recker asked.

"Probably a good part of the day. I've got to dig into Bernal's background, his girlfriend, friends or relatives they might turn to, pour over their phone records, text messages, it all takes time."

"I know. I know the process, you don't have to explain it to me. I was just wondering when."

"Well if you want to help, then it will make everything go quicker."

With nothing else on the agenda, Recker was all too willing to jump in and help. Though Jones was usually faster at digging up the required information, Recker needed anything to keep him busy. Plus, with a police officer's life at stake, Recker wanted to get started on it as soon as possible. Even though he was wanted by them, he really did admire the work and dedication most of them displayed. But Jones was right, this was probably the most delicate case they'd had. Sometimes Recker had to interact with the people he was assigned to help, there was just no way around it. But sometimes the people he was helping had no idea they had a guardian angel watching over them. This would have to be one of those times. The fact the person he was helping was also dangerous, carried a gun, and had the ability to lock him up only complicated things somewhat.

They worked straight through dinner to get the information they needed. Jones tracked down as many friends and relatives of Bernal's he could find, though most of them appeared to be of no use. Outside of his girlfriend, Bernal only disclosed his intentions to one other person, a cousin of his. Through their text messages, Jones concluded that whatever was being planned, it was going to happen quickly. The problem was, Bernal didn't give an exact date or time for when he was going to execute his plan. The other problem was, Bernal didn't have a known address. Though Recker and Jones assumed Bernal might have been staying with his girlfriend, they couldn't say for sure. It would require Recker staking out her place. But if Bernal was staying elsewhere, such as a motel, Recker could be wasting his time at the girlfriend's residence and Bernal might enact his plan without Recker even being in the picture. The only other option was to follow Perez around, and that was deemed too dangerous. If Perez got the slightest hint he was being followed, who knows what might've happened, not to mention following a police patrol car for half the day wasn't exactly an ideal situation. Jones couldn't find any digital traces of Bernal anywhere, such as credit cards being used, or through online social media websites, so he assumed his subject was sticking with cash transactions and deliberately keeping a low profile. It would make finding him much more difficult.

5

———

Recker had been staking out the row home of Bernal's girlfriend for two days without seeing a single sign of the man he was looking for. He'd seen the girlfriend come and go multiple times, but unless Bernal was hiding inside the house, Recker had to assume that he wasn't coming and they had to come up with a new strategy.

Recker pulled out his phone to call his partner. "I dunno, David, this seems like a waste of time."

"Well, right now, the only other options are sitting on the cousin or tailing Perez and I'm not sure how viable either of those are either."

"Yeah, well, I gotta do something. Just sitting here watching the wind blow isn't accomplishing anything."

"I understand but right now it's all we have. Bernal's kept an extremely low profile since being let out of jail," Jones said.

As Recker sat there watching the house, listening to Jones, he was also thinking of alternatives. Suddenly a new idea came to him. It might be considered risky, but without knowing what time frame Bernal was working on, he didn't want to waste more time than he already had.

"David, I'll call you back. I'm gonna try something."

"That sounds extremely vague," Jones said. "Would you like to share before doing something we might regret?"

"I'm gonna talk to the girlfriend."

"Are you sure that's wise?"

"No. But maybe she can tell us something."

"I don't know if it's such a good idea. If he thinks someone's on to him, he might speed things up before we're ready to deal with him."

"Could also scare him away too."

"I would prefer getting more information before confronting anyone," Jones said.

"That's why I'm not gonna ask her anything. I'm gonna have Detective Scarborough do it."

"Oh, dear."

"Keep close tabs on her phone after I'm done."

Recker figured his alter ego might have more luck in getting some kind of useful information out of the girlfriend than if he just approached her on his own as a random citizen. Posing as a police officer was a tactic he'd used successfully several times before. He didn't necessarily expect Maria Guerrero to say anything which would really help him, but hopefully she'd panic at him asking pointed questions and would lead them to Bernal's location. As Recker approached the house, he noticed curtains move on the bow window in the living room. He didn't see a face but assumed someone inside had seen him coming. Guerrero was supposed to be living in the house along with her two kids, but no other adults. Bernal was not the father of the children. As Recker took a few steps up the concrete walkway, he heard a few young kids screaming and playing inside. He knocked on the door and almost immediately the playful screams of the children inside came to a halt. Recker knocked another three times, more forcefully than he did the first time. Knowing they were inside, he patiently waited for someone to answer the door. He knocked a few more times, determined to stand there until he talked to Guerrero. Sensing their visitor wasn't going away, Guerrero finally came to the door.

"Can I help you?" she asked, clearly annoyed in her tone.

Recker took out his badge from his pocket and showed it to her. "Mike Scarborough, Detective Division."

She took a quick glance at the badge, hardly paying much attention to it. "What do you want?"

"I'm looking for Adrian Bernal."

"He's not here."

"Mind if I come in and check?"

"Not without a warrant you're not."

"Do you know where he may be at?"

"No, I have no idea."

"Aren't you his girlfriend?" Recker asked.

"Yeah, so?"

"And you don't know where he's at? Where he's living? Working? Anything?"

"Adrian comes and goes as he pleases. It's his own business, not yours. And he's not working right now. Nobody's exactly beating down his door to offer him a job. One of the perks of our penal system."

"He's been out for, what, a month now?"

"Yeah, and your point?"

"In the time he's been out you haven't seen him, talked to him, nothing?"

"I've met him at a couple bars or whatever," Guerrero said.

"Which ones?"

"I forget the names. He picked me up. Never been to any of them before."

"What kind of car's he driving?"

"Beats me. What I know about cars you could stick in your hat."

Recker let out a smile, amused by the runaround. "Well I need to talk to him and I'd appreciate your help in locating him."

"What do you want him for?" she asked.

"Just some routine questions. There's an investigation we have going on involving some people we think he might have known before, maybe had dealings with," Recker said.

"You're wasting your time. After what he's been through, if you think he's gonna help you guys with anything, you got another thing coming."

"Well, that may be, but I still need to locate and talk to him."

"Good luck with it."

"Did you know him before he was sent up this last time?" Recker asked.

"Yeah, why?"

"So, you remember the arresting officer?"

Guerrero looked at him kind of funny, wondering why he would ask such a question. She hesitated before answering. "No. I don't remember. Why?"

"Well we received an anonymous tip that Officer Perez, the officer who arrested Adrian, may be the subject of some sort of retaliation because of the arrest."

"I wouldn't know anything about that," Guerrero said, shaking her head violently.

"So where would Adrian be right now?"

"I told you I don't know."

"Are you aware, if something happens to Officer Perez, and it's found out you knew something about this before it happens, you can be charged as an accessory to murder? Did you know that?"

"Yes. I know," she said defiantly.

"Be a shame for your kids to grow up without a mother," Recker said, hoping to scare her into some type of admission. "Kids visiting a parent in prison, especially a mother, is never a pretty sight. You might wanna think about it."

"I don't have to think about anything. Are we done?" Guerrero asked, putting a hand on the edge of the door.

"For now. I might be back though. This was more of a courtesy. Maybe next time I'll have a search warrant."

"Great. Thanks."

Guerrero then slammed the door as Recker turned to leave. Though she stuck to her guns and didn't reveal anything which would lead to Bernal directly, Recker felt like his trick worked. He thought she seemed rattled and flustered and there was no doubt in his mind, within minutes she would be calling her boyfriend to inform him the police were just there. Recker walked back to his car and just sat in it for a few minutes, just in case Bernal was actually inside the house. He called Jones to let him know his impersonation was over.

"How did your acting go?" Jones asked.

"Fabulous. Maybe after London I should've gone to Hollywood."

"Let's not get carried away."

"Anyway, keep tabs on Guerrero's phone. If I'm right, she'll be contacting Bernal any minute now," Recker said.

"Why? What did you do?"

"Just tried to step up the pressure."

"Did she tell you anything?"

"No, she clammed up like nobody's business. But she seemed nervous and eager to get rid of me."

"Who wouldn't be?" Jones joked.

While Jones was doing his thing, Recker started the car and began driving, though he didn't leave the area. He just drove down the street to get a different view of Guerrero's house and make it appear like he was leaving the area. If Bernal was inside, which Recker didn't believe he was, he suspected he might bolt out of the house relatively quickly. The more likely scenario was, Guerrero would call her boyfriend to alert him of Recker's presence and questions. But just in case they had some other system in place, Recker stood by in case Guerrero left the house to tell Bernal in person now the police were on to him. Recker wound up waiting in his spot for another hour without any sign of movement from the house. Nobody was coming or going. He knew nothing was going to come from him sitting there any longer. If they were going to have face-to-face contact, they would've done it by now. The best Recker could hope for now was if Jones was able to track something on his end. Before leaving, Recker gave his partner another call before making the decision to flee the scene.

"I'm about to wrap things up here, there's nothing happening," Recker said. "If Guerrero was going to meet him or warn him, she would've done it by now. You come up with anything?"

"I have, though I can't say it's the break we've been looking for either. Not just yet."

"Well what'd you get?"

"You were right. You spooked Guerrero. Right after you left she called a phone number which I cannot establish a name to, but I can only assume it's Bernal's."

"Burner phone?"

"Most likely. And it's a different number than she's called before so it's likely he has several of them. Or he keeps switching phones. Both of which are entirely plausible," Jones said.

"Smart. Not like the usual dumbbell we come into contact with. Can you still get a trace on it?"

"Well, as you know, most burner phones can still be traced in some way. Though I don't know if I'll be able to get an exact location, I should be able to trace it to the nearest cell tower."

"Lot of good that'll do," Recker said.

"I know. Tracing burners takes a lot more work, and it's not as precise. By the time I can triangulate his general position and figure out where he may be, it's likely he'll be long gone."

"Well, do it anyway. At the very least it's more than we've got now. Maybe if we can figure out where he's been we can figure out where he's going."

"Let's just hope we can figure it out before he enacts his plot on Officer Perez."

"Maybe we should just phone in a tip about Bernal's plans. At least Perez would be aware of it and can keep his head up."

"We can, but you know as well as I do the police get threats all the time," Jones said. "It doesn't mean they can or will do anything. Especially if there's no evidence."

"They don't need evidence. They just need to know the possibility is out there. What about his parole?"

"What about it?"

"He had to put an address down upon release," Recker said.

"It's a dead end. I've already looked into it. He used his girlfriend's address as his residence and he should've already checked in with a parole officer in the last couple of weeks."

"I guess it's checked out?"

"Well there hasn't been an arrest warrant issued so I imagine everything turned up fine on those fronts. Another dead end I'm afraid. Unless he really is living at his girlfriend's house."

"I really don't think so. If he is, he hasn't come up for air in two days. Plus, I doubt she would've made a call after I visited. He would've known if he was stashed in a different room. Who would she have called?"

"Maybe he is living there and was just out when you knocked," Jones said.

"No, no way. I've been sitting here day and night for two days. I would've noticed him coming or going at some point. Or another car at least."

"Unless he snuck out the back."

"The only reason to do that is if you think you're being watched," Recker said.

"And maybe he knows you're there."

"No. I'd stake my reputation on it."

Though Recker wanted to head back to the office, Jones convinced him to stay put for a little longer. There wasn't much he could do at the office and Jones figured he was better served where he was, just in case Bernal made an appearance, even if it was unlikely. After a couple more hours of watching and waiting, without anything to show for it, Jones finally called him with a lead.

"What's up?" Recker asked, hopeful of good news.

"I've tracked him down as far as I can."

"Great. Where is he?"

"Well, his call from Guerrero was bounced off a cell phone tower that is right next to the Cedar Motel," Jones said. "I'm fairly confident that he's likely to be in one of those rooms. Well, I should say confident that's where he was. Whether he's still there is an entirely different matter."

"I'm on my way there now," Recker said, driving away from Guerrero's house.

"I'll let you know if I pick up anything else."

"By the way, how many rooms does the motel have?"

Recker listened while Jones clicked around his keyboard. "Looks like twenty."

"Shouldn't make it too difficult for Detective Scarborough," Recker said.

The Cedar Motel wasn't too far away from Guerrero's house. Recker got there in under twenty minutes. Once he got there his first stop was the management's office. When Recker walked in, he saw a balding, older man sitting behind the desk doing a crossword puzzle.

"Help ya?" the man asked.

Recker took out his badge and showed it to him. "Looking for a man. We believe he's been staying here and wondering if you can confirm it."

"Oh. Got a picture?"

"Sure do," Recker said, taking out his phone to show Bernal's photo.

The man grunted as he looked it over. "Yeah. He's been here."

"Have any problems with him or anything?"

"Nope."

"He still here?"

"As far as I know. He hasn't officially checked out yet."

"What room's he in?" Recker asked.

"Fourteen."

"Thanks."

"Wait," the man said, getting nervous about what was to happen.

"Yeah?"

"You're not gonna break the door down or anything or get in a gunfight are you?"

"I dunno. Why?"

"Well I just don't want the room to get messed up. Getting repairs done is a pain in the you know what."

"I'll do my best," Recker said, not the least bit concerned.

"Wait, wait, wait... here's a spare key to the room. At least don't kick the door in, huh?"

Recker couldn't help but smile and let out a laugh. "Fine. The door will stay intact. Can't guarantee about bullet holes in the wall though."

"Great. Of all the cops who could come through here, I gotta get Wyatt Earp," the man whispered.

"Stay here in case there's shooting," Recker said, exiting the office.

There were only a few cars in the parking lot, and all the rooms weren't currently rented, so Recker couldn't be sure whether Bernal was there or not. Even if he was, Recker had no idea what kind of car he was driving. He quickly walked past each room, clinging to the brick wall lining the building, until he got to room fourteen. Recker tried looking through the window into the room, but the curtains weren't pulled back and he couldn't even get the tiniest view in there. He squatted and walked underneath the window to avoid his shadow from being seen crossing it from inside the room. If Bernal was in there, Recker knew it was likely he was going to be drawing gunfire the moment he opened the door.

With the key still in his hand, he put it in the hole of the handle and unlocked the door. He tried to do it as slowly and quietly as possible, but he thought it was unlikely that someone on the inside wouldn't have heard him coming. To give himself better odds of surviving an initial flurry of bullets, Recker squatted again, figuring his best chance at eluding gunfire was to dive into the room. He thought it best to dive in quickly before Bernal got impatient and started blasting at the door before it opened. He turned the handle of the door and violently pushed it open so it slammed against the wall. With his gun drawn, he dove into the room, quickly looking for a target. Everything was quiet. There were no guns firing, no bullets piercing through walls, no commotion of any kind.

Recker got up and took a look around the room, even checking under the bed. These motel rooms were pretty small, and there weren't many places someone could hide, even if they wanted to. There was a small kitchen area off the main space and the only other room was a bathroom. Recker took a look in there as well, but like the rest of the place, came up empty. At least the manager would be pleased his room didn't get shot up. Recker then searched through the room, looking for the smallest of clues to help to tell him where Bernal was headed, or where else he might have been. Anything at all. A piece of paper with a name or address written on it, a crumpled up paper in the trash bin, something he might have forgotten or left behind in a drawer, anything. But it was no use. The room was spotless. Recker even looked in the refrigerator, but there wasn't a single thing in there. It was a lost cause. There was nothing to be learned there. He called Jones to inform him of his findings.

"Looks like Bernal's already gone," Recker said.

"Well I can't say I'm shocked. I was afraid this would be the result."

"I've looked through this room several times for some kind of lead but there's nothing here."

"Mr. Bernal does appear to be good at hiding his tracks," Jones said. "I have to say I'm a little surprised he's been this difficult to find. Nothing in his background suggests he moves in the shadows or that he's capable of being this deceptive."

"People can surprise you with what they can pull off when they have something major like murder at stake."

6

———————

Recker and Jones were in the office, trying everything within reason to try to find out where Bernal may have been hiding. Beyond what they were doing with the computer, which wasn't turning up much, Recker knew he had to put everything at his disposal in play. It would mean calling in some favors.

"I think it's time to get Tyrell involved," Recker said.

"You think he can help?"

"When has Tyrell not been able to help? He knows these streets far better than you and I do. He might know a friend of a friend of a friend or something."

"It surely wouldn't hurt."

Recker immediately dialed Tyrell's number, who picked up on the second ring. "You got anything going on right now?" Recker asked.

"At this exact minute?"

"Well, relatively soon."

"Depends. Whatcha need?"

"Information. I'm looking for a guy."

"I might be able to help you," Tyrell said.

"Guy I'm looking for is named Adrian Bernal."

"Adrian Bernal," Tyrell said, racking his brain. "Bernal. Bernal."

Recker hoped by the silence it meant Tyrell could remember him. "Know him?"

"Nah, I don't think I know the cat."

"You think you can put the word out or find out about him?"

"Depends on what you want. Depends if you're looking to find him and have a talk or you're looking to find him and take him out. You want one of those hush-hush deals?"

"Yeah. He can't know I'm coming or else it'll scare him off," Recker said.

"All right, I gotcha. What's he wanted for? He dangerous?"

"He's looking to kill a cop, Tyrell. I'd say he's pretty dangerous."

"Oh, man, that's bad news. All right, I'll put my minions on it and let you know if I find out anything. How soon's all this going down?"

"To be honest, I have no idea. The quicker you can get something, the better off we'll be."

"You know it. I'll get back to you."

Recker hung up, putting the phone back in his pants pocket. "Hopefully it pays off," Jones said.

"You think he can pull this off by himself?" Recker

said.

"Who? Tyrell?"

"No. Bernal. I mean, taking out a cop requires precision planning, not to mention acquiring weapons."

"Why not? You could."

"Comparing a street thug to me isn't exactly a fair comparison."

"True. You also may be putting too much thought into it. Your level of planning into something like this might not be equal to his. If you do a hit, you're looking at exit strategies, plans, the environment, onlookers, etc. He may not be interested in any of that. He may only be looking at killing Perez without worrying about how he's getting away, if he is at all," Jones said. "Plus, I'm sure he's well aware of who he can go to for a weapon."

It didn't take long for Tyrell to find something that would be useful. About three hours after getting the nod from Recker, he called back with his findings.

"Hey, you're in luck," Tyrell said.

"What'd you find out?" Recker asked.

"Looks like your man's got himself a few guns."

"How do you know?"

"Who's the major gun supplier in this city?"

"Jeremiah."

"Exactly. I got word to Jeremiah to see if he knew who this cat was and they said they did business with the dude."

"Did you find out what the exact transaction was?" Recker asked.

"Nah, they wasn't talking too much about specifics.

From what I could tell it was more than one though."

"Find out anything else?"

"No, not yet. But Jeremiah might have more info for you if you're of a mind."

"Why?"

"Well they wanted to know why I was asking about Bernal," Tyrell said. "So, I told them I was asking on your behalf."

"That was kind of you."

"Hey, you know, when you start asking someone like Jeremiah about his business, you better be prepared to have some answers for him as to why you're asking," Tyrell said with a laugh. "And the only thing I had was, you wanted to know."

"Don't worry about it, it's fine."

"Well anyway, Jeremiah's willing to talk to you about it."

"He's got something else on his mind, I take it," Recker said.

"Yeah, sounded like it."

"Know what it is?"

"No, but, I dunno, he seems different lately," Tyrell said.

"Different how?"

"I don't know how to explain it. He just seems jumpier. Like he's restless or something."

"That doesn't sound very encouraging."

"Maybe he's getting ready for a war with Vincent."

"What makes you think that? Hear something about it?"

"Nothing specific. Just, Jeremiah's been recruiting hard. Usually when men like him start looking for more soldiers, they got something specific in mind. Like taking more territory or something."

"Or maybe he just fears Vincent's getting too big and he'll make a move on him first," Recker said.

"Could be. Anyway, if you wanna meet with him, I'll let him know you're coming."

"What time?"

"He said one hour."

"Usual spot?"

"Same spot as always."

"I'll be there."

"Good news?" Jones asked, overhearing part of the conversation.

"Could be. Looks like Bernal went to Jeremiah for some guns."

"I take it you're meeting with him to see if he has anything else to offer?"

"Yeah."

"What was that stuff about Jeremiah and Vincent?"

"I don't know. Tyrell said Jeremiah seemed jumpy lately. Maybe he's getting worried about Vincent getting too big a stake of the city."

"Possible."

"Yeah, well, doesn't really matter to me. I'll be back."

Recker immediately left the office to head to the meeting with Jeremiah. It'd been a while since they had one. The last time was after Recker killed Bellomi, and Jeremiah wondered if The Silencer was working with

Vincent, after the mob boss publicly displayed the dead body of Mancini to announce he was taking on more territory. By the time Recker got to the area of the meeting house, he was a half hour early, but he didn't mind sitting for a while. He parked down the street as it wasn't wise to sit in front of a place Jeremiah owns for too long if you're not conducting business at the time. It'd give the impression he was running surveillance on them. And if it was the case, then whoever's sitting there might as well get their gun out, because Jeremiah's men would be, and they'd come out shooting. It gave Recker time to think and look around. It'd been a year since he'd been to the house, or the area in general, but it didn't look like anything had changed. Once the time came near, Recker pulled down the street, parking in front of the house. He saw the same burly man standing by the front door as usual.

"Good to see you're still kicking around," Recker said as he walked past him. "Don't bother to show me in, I know my way around."

The man stood pat, not really appreciating Recker's sense of humor. If he had his way, he probably would've tried working Recker's face over a couple of times. But those weren't Jeremiah's wishes, so his desires would have to go unfulfilled. As Recker walked into the living room of the boarded-up house, he saw his host sitting in the chair in the middle of the room. Recker sat down across from him and looked around, seeing that they were alone.

"When you gonna get around to decorating this place?" Recker said.

"You know, I think you say the same thing every time

you come here," Jeremiah said.

"Well, I guess I figure one of these times you'll start listening."

"Still crazy as ever I see."

"Don't wanna ruin my reputation."

"I heard you left town for a while. Too much heat on you?"

"No, nothing I couldn't handle. Just had to take care of some business elsewhere for a while. I'm back for good now."

"Glad to hear it."

"Are you?"

"Yeah. Why wouldn't I be?" Jeremiah asked.

"I dunno. Just checking. Not everybody's so happy to see me."

"I can understand how it is. Enough of the pleasantries though. I hear you wanna know about this guy I sold some guns to."

"Yeah. Adrian Bernal."

"Why? What's it to you?"

"I just have an interest in it. What'd you sell him?"

"Handgun and an assault rifle."

"You know what he wants them for?" Recker asked, not sure how involved he was.

"Yeah. He wants to kill a cop. At least that's what he told me. Why you looking for him?"

"I've been hired to stop him."

"What would you wanna do that for? As far as I'm concerned, one less cop is good for everybody."

"Well, my employer thinks otherwise."

"I'd have thought this would be a case you'd turn down," Jeremiah said. "Since when'd you get so chummy with the cops? I'd think you'd be happy about one less cop hunting you."

"Nah. Not my thing. I just go where the money is."

"Yeah, I bet."

"So you know where Bernal's heading or when he's planning on doing this thing?"

"Maybe I do. It's nothing I can talk to you about though."

"Why not?"

"It'd be bad for business."

"How you figure?" Recker said.

"People come to me 'cause they know I'll have the merchandise they're looking for. They know they can trust me once they get it," Jeremiah said. "Now, how would it look if I sold people out after I sell them the goods? My reputation takes a hit and I start to lose business."

"You're assuming someone would find out about it. You know I'm certainly not gonna spill the beans. After I kill him, who's gonna know?"

"And you're assuming you live and he doesn't. What happens if it's reversed, or he finds out about it?"

"You really think some small-time hood's gonna get one over on me?"

"What, you think you're gonna live forever?" Jeremiah asked, smiling. "Time's gonna come for all of us. You and me both. We're not any different."

"Probably true," Recker said, confused by his host's intentions. "If you're not willing to help me find this guy, I have to wonder what I'm doing here then. I mean, what was the point of this? The only thing you told me was what weapons you sold him. Not really much of a revelation, I could've guessed as much."

"Because I got some other things to discuss with you. Wasn't sure you'd come otherwise."

Intrigued, Recker sat up a little straighter in his chair. "And just what might those other things be?"

"Where your allegiances lie."

"My allegiances? They lie at the same place they always have. With myself."

"Nah, you're gonna have a dog in this fight. You have to," Jeremiah said.

"You know, I'm sure we both have things we need to get done so why don't you stop talking in circles and tell me what it is you really want," Recker said.

"Things seem to be heating up between me and Vincent."

"Really? I haven't heard anything about it."

"Mostly low-key stuff right now."

"Is that why you've been recruiting?"

Jeremiah smiled, impressed his visitor seemed on top of his game. "That's what I like about you. Whether you're here or not, you always know what's going on, always got one ear on the street."

"So, what's been happening?"

"Like I said, just small stuff, but it's adding up. Some of Vincent's men have been seen in my territory from time to time. I can only assume it means they're scouting things out."

"Could mean anything," Recker said, not jumping to any conclusions. "Doesn't necessarily means he wants to start a war."

"You know what his intentions are?"

"Haven't the foggiest."

"If things happen, I wanna know which side you're on," Jeremiah said.

"I'm not on anybody's side. I've done business with you. I've done business with him. I'm on even terms with both of you. I don't have a dog in this fight."

"A man like you can really tip the scales, tip the balance as to who's got the upper hand, who has the most power."

"Not taking sides," Recker said.

"Maybe I can persuade you."

"Before you get all hot and bothered with what you think is going on, why don't you actually request a meeting with Vincent and talk? Then you can get everything out in the open."

"You think he's really gonna tell me if he's trying to move in? All it'd do is give him a better target."

"I think you're worrying about nothing."

Jeremiah leaned forward in his chair as he was about to drop his next bombshell. "I need to know you're with me."

"I don't know how many times I can tell you I'm not. I'm not with anybody. The only person I'm with is me. If you and Vincent go to war, it's on you guys. I won't get involved."

Jeremiah's eyebrows dropped as a scowl came over his

face. He looked at Recker with mean intent, not pleased at The Silencer's stance. He was hoping to convince Recker to join his side before trying to blackmail him into it. But a man like Recker could give either side the edge in an upcoming war between the two parties, and Jeremiah wasn't about to let Vincent swing him over to his.

"I was hoping you wouldn't take such an adversarial tone," Jeremiah said.

"There's nothing adversarial about it. I'm just not taking sides."

"I was hoping you'd fall in with me on your own and I wouldn't have to do this, but it seems you're not giving me much choice. I can't afford to let you walk out of here without knowing you're with me. If you fall into Vincent's hands, then that's on me."

"You're not listening to me," Recker said.

"I think I am."

Recker was starting to get a little antsy at the way the conversation was going. It seemed to be going in the wrong direction. The manner in which Jeremiah was talking was making Recker feel uneasy, like he had to start looking around for some unwelcome guests to come into the room who might take some shots at him. Luckily, he was armed and Jeremiah didn't have him frisked for weapons when he got there. Of course, he might not have been as willing to hand over his guns to Jeremiah's crew as he was to Vincent's. For whatever reason, he was always more trusting of Vincent than he was of Jeremiah. Though they were both equally as dangerous, Recker always considered Jeremiah more of a loose cannon, someone who was more likely to double cross him than Vincent was. His suspicions were about to be proven correct.

"I'm not waiting around anymore for Vincent to make the next move," Jeremiah said. "We both know he's eventually gonna make a play for what I got. Maybe it's today, maybe it's next month, maybe it's not for another year. But we both know it's gonna happen. I figure it's better to go on the offensive and hit him before he does it to me."

"No concern of mine," Recker said.

"I want your help."

"You're not getting it."

"I think I will."

Jeremiah reached into his pocket, causing Recker to squirm in his seat in anticipation of a gun being pointed at him. Recker reached into his coat and put his hand on the handle of his gun in case he needed to react quickly. Jeremiah pulled out a piece of paper and looked at it for a minute, causing Recker to relax his hand away from his weapon.

"I understand you know her," Jeremiah said, holding the paper out in front of him.

With a concerned look on his face, Recker glared at his host, before grabbing the piece of paper. He let his eyes drop down to it, horrified at what he saw. It was a picture of Mia taped to the sheet of paper, with her name and address written underneath her photo. Recker, not wanting to admit he knew her, tried to play it off. He shrugged and handed the paper back to Jeremiah.

"So? Who is she?" Recker asked.

"You're saying you don't know her?"

"Not to my knowledge. Why? What's this about?"

A sinister smile overtook Jeremiah's face as he took out another piece of paper, this one having nine more pictures stapled to it. Once again, he handed it over to his surprised guest. Recker quickly looked the pictures over and saw several pictures of him and Mia sitting together at the hospital cafeteria. It looked to him like the photos had been taken several months ago, probably just before Recker left for Detroit. His blood started boiling. Recker took his eyes off the pictures and peered up at Jeremiah, wanting to extract his revenge on him by filling him full of holes.

"Now that's the face of a man I need," Jeremiah said.

"What is this about?"

"So you admit now you know her?"

"Met her at the hospital when I was having some work done," Recker said. "Talked to her for a little bit, nothing came of it."

"Looked a little cozier than a chat."

Tired of the conversation, Recker wasn't handing the pictures back and put them in his pocket as he started to get up.

"That's all right. You can keep those," Jeremiah said. "I got copies made."

Recker sat back in his seat, anger clearly visible on his face. "What do you want?"

Jeremiah threw his hands up, looking like he hadn't a care in the world. "I keep telling you. I want you working for me."

"Are you trying to blackmail me?"

"You can call it whatever you want. I know where this girl works. I know where she lives. I got people tailing her. If you care anything at all about her, you'll play ball."

"Or else?"

"Or else she's fish food, man."

"You really think this is a good idea? Making an enemy out of me?" Recker asked angrily.

"The thing is, it's not what I'm doing. We're gonna be partners. You help me out. I'll help you out."

"I don't need any help from you."

"You help me get rid of Vincent and the girl lives. It's as simple as that," Jeremiah said, confident in his actions.

"Until you want something else from me and you take someone else hostage to try to get my assistance."

"All I want is Vincent. If you'd just said yes to begin with, I wouldn't have to go through these extreme and drastic measures. And if you have any thoughts to putting a bullet in my head before you leave here, just know this; if my man's watching her doesn't hear from me, he's got instructions to put two in her chest."

"And just how do you propose doing this takeover of yours?" Recker asked.

"You set up a meeting with him. I don't care what you tell him, say whatever you want, just get him and his top guys together. Then take them out."

"Just like that, huh? Just get them together and kill them all?"

"You set it up, you tell us where it's gonna be, I'll have men already waiting there inside the building. Then I'll have more guys swoop in and surround the place," Jeremiah said. "There'll be nowhere for him to escape."

"And the odds of me escaping this crossfire exchange?"

"That's why you should hurry up and get it done so you can get to ducking."

"And your time frame for all this?" Recker said.

"Let's make it within the next week or so. I don't like long setups. Too many things can change, people start to get stupid ideas in their heads, like maybe there's other ways around doing what needs to be done. The quicker the better. This will also be the last time we meet face to face until the job is done. Just in case there's ideas about taking me out and rescuing her before the job is completed."

Recker reached back into his coat and pulled out the pictures of him and Mia, looking them over. "How'd you come across these?"

"Just dumb luck really. I had some acquaintances of mine who happened to be at the hospital," Jeremiah said. "They just happened to be in the cafeteria when they recognized you. They saw you sitting with a pretty girl who looked like she worked there and started snapping some pictures. They showed them to me and I thought I needed to find out who this girl was. She your girlfriend?"

"No. Just a friend."

"But an important friend. I can dig it, man. I got some pretty friends like her too."

"So, what, you've just been sitting on these for a few months, waiting for the right time to spring them on me?"

"Something like that."

"So, are you on board?"

"Guess I don't have much choice, do I?"

Jeremiah smiled, knowing he had his dangerous friend over a barrel. With their business concluded, Recker stood up to leave. Jeremiah extended his hand to cement their deal, which Recker spurned, instead choosing to ignore his new business partner as he left the premises. Jeremiah followed him to the door and watched Recker get into his car and drive away.

"Is he playing ball?" one of Jeremiah's men asked.

"Oh yeah."

"You really think we can trust him?"

"As long as we got the leverage. Put a couple more men on his lady friend, just in case he gets any funny ideas."

As Recker was driving, he tried to think of how he was getting out of his predicament. Nobody was going to blackmail him and get away with it. He certainly wasn't getting involved in Vincent and Jeremiah's feud and he definitely wasn't going to kill anyone for them, or do their dirty work. But he was kicking himself for getting Mia involved. Even though it wasn't his doing, she was in danger because of her relationship to him. He just had to figure out how he was going to get her out of it. He was going to have to figure out a way to protect her while also permanently getting rid of the problem. And the problem was Jeremiah. If he threatened her once, he'd do it again. In order to protect Mia, he was not only going to have to shield her from whoever was tailing her, Recker was going to have to kill Jeremiah.

By the slamming of the office door, Jones could tell Recker wasn't in the best of moods. He assumed the meeting with Jeremiah didn't produce the results they were looking for. Little did he know Recker was about to spring a new problem on him. Recker was so consumed with rage, and stewing over his problems, he didn't even bother to let Jones know what was going on. And with the news Jeremiah had sprung on him, Recker had almost completely forgotten about why he went there to begin with. Ever since he was told Mia was being used as a bargaining chip, Recker hadn't had a single thought about Adrian Bernal. Jones greeted him as he came in, though Recker didn't acknowledge him. Jones assumed he didn't hear him, as was sometimes the case when Recker was deep in thought. Usually Jones either kept pestering him until he responded or he just left Recker alone until he came around. Considering Recker kept pacing around the room, causing Jones to lose his concentration, he began pestering his partner until he snapped out of whatever funk he was in.

"Didn't go well, I take it?" Jones asked.

"Huh?"

"No answers?"

"What?" Recker said, not really comprehending what was being said to him.

"Did you find out anything?"

"What?" Recker asked, still pacing, hearing something, but not concentrating on the words.

Finally, Jones figured he had to go to extremes to get his friend's attention. He stood up and started waving his arms around, eventually succeeding in catching Recker's attention.

Recker stopped and looked at Jones curiously. "What are you doing?"

"Well, considering I've been talking to you for five minutes without a reply, I was starting to get desperate."

"Oh. Sorry."

"Good thing you responded. If you didn't notice then I was beginning to think the only thing you'd notice was if I stripped down to my boxers."

"Uh, yeah, don't do that."

"Desperate times call for desperate measures."

"Right. So what were you trying to talk to me about?"

"I was asking how your meeting with Jeremiah went," Jones said.

"Oh. Horrible. Couldn't have gone worse."

"Didn't have anything on Bernal?"

"No, not really. Just told me he sold him a couple guns. Nothing more."

"Didn't know more or just didn't want to reveal more?" Jones asked.

"Said it was bad for business to inform on his clients."

Recker looked away as he thought about Mia. Jones could tell something else was on his mind. He didn't think Recker would look so despondent just because he came away from a meeting without any new information. Not unless it was something personal. Whatever it was, it didn't seem like something that Recker was too interested in sharing.

"Mike, what is it?"

"Huh?" Recker asked, hearing Jones' voice, but not his words.

"Something else is bothering you. I can tell. It's not just about Bernal, is it?"

"No."

"Something from your meeting with Jeremiah or something else entirely?"

Knowing that a picture was worth a thousand words, Recker dug into his pocket and took out the photos he took from Jeremiah. As he looked them over, Jones could tell he was troubled by whatever it was. Recker briefly looked at them, then handed them to Jones. As the professor browsed through the pictures, he now understood what Recker's problem was, though he hadn't yet learned of how big the issue actually was.

"So, Jeremiah knows about you and Mia?"

"Worse," Recker said.

"You're holding something back. What else aren't you saying?"

"Jeremiah's using Mia as a bargaining chip. He's got people tailing her."

"Oh," Jones said, realizing the severity of the situation. "For what purpose? What does he want?"

"He's using her to get me to work for him."

"To do what?"

"He wants me to take out Vincent for him," Recker said, drawing a surprised look from his friend.

"That's uh... I don't understand why he needs you involved."

"He thinks that at some point, whether soon or not, Vincent's going to try and take over his territory. Instead of waiting and being on the defensive, he wants to get out in front and take Vincent by surprise."

"I still don't see how that involves you."

"Because he knows I've dealt with Vincent before. He thinks I have Vincent's trust and can get a meeting with him, where he wouldn't suspect anything," Recker said. "And then I take him out."

"And why does he need to involve Mia?"

"Because I told him I wouldn't do it. I said whatever they do is between them. Then he showed me those," Recker said, nodding at the pictures. "He said he's got men on her all day. That if I don't take Vincent out, that Mia would be killed."

"Well that certainly is troubling, isn't it?"

"Troubling is hardly the word for it."

"So, what are you going to do?" Jones said.

"Well I'm not killing anybody for Jeremiah and definitely not Vincent. I don't have anything against him and nobody's gonna blackmail me into doing something like that for them."

"Just don't do it then. You can get to Mia before Jeremiah realizes it."

"The problem would then be what do I do with her? She has a boyfriend, she works, I can't just stuff her someplace for who knows how long. And I can't just sit there with her indefinitely either."

"I see what you mean. When does he expect you to do this?"

"Within the week," Recker said.

"Doesn't give us much time."

"No, it doesn't. Especially when we still have another pressing matter to attend to."

"Bernal. I almost forgot how urgent that was."

"I can't protect Mia and look for Bernal at the same time. Because if I take Mia off the grid, even for a couple weeks, and don't take out Vincent, I've declared war on Jeremiah and his men."

"Well, he'd have taken the first shot."

"Doesn't really matter, does it? In his mind, I'd be going back on the deal."

"Or you continue after Bernal until you find him. While you're doing that, I'll stay with Mia," Jones said.

"It's a nice gesture, David, but I don't think it'll work. If they see someone staying with her, like a bodyguard, they'll know something's up. And they'll come after you.

You won't be able to defend either one of you against Jeremiah's crew."

"What about Tyrell? Or even Vincent? No doubt he'd be thankful for the news of the impending assassination. I'm sure he'd be willing to supply protection for Mia as a measure of thanks."

"I don't think Tyrell can be of help on this one," Recker said. "Every time he's helped us on something, he didn't have ties to who we were looking for. He does with Jeremiah. He's one of his biggest customers. As friendly as we are with Tyrell, I don't think he'll want to mess with where his bread is buttered."

"You forget, money is not an issue for us. I can give him enough money to last him for years. Even send his brother to college. The least we can do is ask."

"I still don't know. Even if he's willing to help, he's a major resource for us," Recker said, resisting the idea. "He's got connections, he knows people, if others found out he went against Jeremiah, they may turn against him. He may wind up being not as valuable to us. He might even end up dead."

"I would say Mia's life trumps any possible future connections Tyrell may have in store for us. If he's a well of information that dries up then so be it. This is an all hands on deck situation."

"I know. There's just... there's gotta be another way."

"I'm assuming the only way this ends is with Jeremiah being dead, correct?" Jones asked.

"Has to. Otherwise Mia will always be a target."

"I know. I'm not railing against it or anything. I understand this is the only way. What if you take out Jeremiah, and as you're doing it, I'll make sure Mia's safe? We'd have to time it precisely."

"No, won't work. Jeremiah won't meet with me again until Vincent's dead. He's afraid of something bad happening."

"OK. What about my suggestion of having Vincent help?"

"Up to now Vincent and I have been on good terms," Recker said. "But it may not always be the case. Up to now, Jeremiah and I were on good terms. Things can change in a heartbeat. I don't want to get her out from Jeremiah's grasps just to put her in Vincent's."

"He already knows about her though. We both know it."

"You were the one way back when who told me we should be cautious in dealing with him and asking for favors. We've already done it one too many times. Eventually he's gonna ask for a receipt on those."

"What if we don't tell Vincent anything? We just ask for his support in taking out Jeremiah. He obviously wouldn't be opposed to that."

Recker let out a laugh, amused at the prospect of taking out Vincent's competition yet again. "Kind of funny, isn't it?"

"What is?" Jones asked, not seeing the humor.

"When we first started this, I said I wasn't going to help any criminals. Wasn't gonna help them, wasn't gonna save them."

"Things happen we always can't envision."

"Just weird how things work out sometimes. If I take out Jeremiah, it means I'd have eliminated two major criminal organizations in this city. When I arrived, there were three main players here. Once Jeremiah's gone, there will only be one."

"Well the other two only have themselves to blame for their downfalls."

"Yeah," Recker said, shaking his head. "It's just hard to fathom how much I helped shake things out here. Vincent had two enemies when I got here. I already took out one. Now I'm about to take out the other. Both gone without him having to lift a finger."

"Well if it makes you feel any better, you probably helped avoid more bloodshed."

"How'd you figure?"

"Well it's true you helped shrink things down, but it was always going to happen, anyway. It was inevitable. We both know it. You taking out Vincent's competition isn't something that wouldn't have occurred if you hadn't been here. Those three factions would have had their war for more power at some point. You just sped things up. And you did it without the war. If those three factions had erupted, who knows how many innocent people would have gotten caught up in their dealings?"

"Yeah, I guess so."

"Why don't you just tell Vincent that Jeremiah wants you to kill him then let things take their course? Let them deal with each other," Jones said.

"Nice in theory but it doesn't exactly help Mia," Recker said. "Vincent's not just gonna find Jeremiah in a matter of minutes. And don't forget how Vincent likes to meticulously plan things out. He likes to play the slow game. As soon as Jeremiah gets wind of Vincent planning action against him, and that I helped him, or that I didn't kill him myself, he'll put a bullet in Mia's head."

"You're right."

"No, what I gotta do is protect Mia, kill Jeremiah, and find Bernal. And I gotta do it all at the same time."

"It's a good thing we came back," Jones said. "Who else would've been able to handle all this?"

"Yeah, nothing like coming back with a bang."

"Not to complicate matters even more, but based upon your last conversation with Mia, how do you propose to protect her considering she probably doesn't even want to see you?"

"You sure like to pile on, huh?"

"Well it is something of a quandary, is it not?"

"Umm, well," Recker said, stuttering as he tried to think of a solution. "I guess I've got two choices."

"Which are?"

"I either protect her covertly so she doesn't know I'm there. Or... I sneak up behind her, throw her in my car and kidnap her, taking her to a secure location until this matter's settled."

"Hmm," Jones said. "I have to think the second way may not go over so well."

"Yeah."

"You also have another problem?"

"You really are a bearer of bad news, aren't you?"

"Well, since you said it, it reminds me of the fact we

don't have a secure location. We've never protected some-body this way before, by hiding them somewhere. We've always done it lurking in the shadows. Without their knowledge until the last possible second."

"I know. Any suggestions or ideas?" Recker asked, ready to listen to just about anything.

Jones thought for a few seconds, but nothing came to him. "Not at the moment."

Recker continued thinking, and after a couple minutes of silence between them, finally came up with what he thought was a good solution. He was positive Jones wouldn't like it though. The professor could tell Recker had thought of something by the little grin on his face and the way he was staring into nothingness. It was a sure indication he'd come up with something.

"I almost hate to ask," Jones said, observing his part-ner's face. "What are you scheming in that head of yours?"

"You really wanna know?"

Jones closed his eyes and sighed, knowing there was no good answer to the question. "I do, though I have a feeling I may not like the answer."

"Well, you're wrong about us not having a secure loca-tion," Recker said. "We do have one. We use it all the time."

Jones tilted his head as he tried to wrap his head around what Recker was talking about. Then, after a few seconds, his eyes almost bulged out of his head and his mouth fell open as he realized what his friend was talking about.

"Please tell me you're not suggesting what I think you are?"

"Can you think of a more secure location than here?" Recker asked.

"Mike, the only people who know about this place are you and I."

"I know. It's perfect."

"But... there's a reason we decided to have a place of business to operate out of which nobody else knew about," Jones said. "If someone else outside of our circle knows of it, then it's no longer effective."

"Mia's not really out of our circle. I mean, she's the closest friend either one of us has."

"Yes, I know, and I know she's trustworthy—"

Recker interrupted. "She could've given us up a long time ago."

"I'm not debating her character."

"Then what are you debating?"

Jones put his hands on his face and rubbed his eyes as he tried to formulate his thoughts into something cogent. "Though I do not believe Mia would ever intentionally give us or our location up, we've now seen several times, whether through her own means or ours, she is a target because of her relationship to us."

"You're worried that six months from now, if she knows our location, she'll show up and lead someone to us who she's not aware of?"

"That is my fear."

"Then we find a new office after this is over. We move somewhere else," Recker said. "I'm sure you can find another spot within the city, or in the suburbs which would work just as well."

Jones turned away from his partner for a minute, instead choosing to concentrate on the computer screen in front of him as he contemplated Recker's request. Knowing it was a lot to ask, Recker kept himself busy for a few minutes by attending to his guns in the cabinet. Though he believed it was the only solution for the time being, he knew it threw Jones for a loop, springing something of that magnitude on him suddenly. After briefly considering the pros and cons of the situation, and realizing they were losing time on all fronts, Jones finally rendered his decision.

"I guess there really is no other decision to make right now, is there?" Jones said.

Recker closed the gun cabinet and shook his head. "No, not really."

"We got into this business to help people. And no one is more important than Mia," Jones said, looking around the room. "And as you said, this is just an office, nothing more really."

"I know this place holds sentimental value for you since this is where we started everything. But in the end, it's just a building."

"I suppose you're right. The bigger question is how you intend to get Mia here without Jeremiah's men knowing about it."

"Oh, I have a few ideas," Recker said.

"Why does that not surprise me?"

"Do these ideas involve killing anyone or just losing them?"

"Well, if they're dead then they'd be considered lost, wouldn't they?"

"Yes, I suppose they would in some sort of logic."

"I'm not as concerned about the men watching her. I'm more concerned about her," Recker said. "I'm not exactly her favorite person right now."

"Well if you explain the situation, I'm sure she would understand."

"Getting my foot in the door to explain it might be the tricky part. Maybe you might have better luck."

Jones looked at him strangely, hardly believing his ears. "Are you afraid to talk to her?"

"What? Pffft. Don't be ridiculous. Of course I'm not afraid to talk to her."

Recker may have insisted he wasn't apprehensive about talking to Mia, but his body language said otherwise. He was shifting in his stance and his eyes were dancing about the room, not wanting to look at Jones as they talked about it. The longer the professor looked at him, the more amazed he was. Recker would rather face ten guys with guns in a locked room than face one woman who rightfully chewed him out. Jones couldn't believe it. He never thought he'd see the day when Recker actually appeared afraid to do something, especially something as trivial as talking to someone who he had feelings for.

"You are," Jones said again. "You're afraid of her giving you the business again."

Recker put his hand up to debate the point but quickly

put it down, seeing as he really didn't have a leg to stand on. Jones was right. Not necessarily about being afraid to talk to Mia, but him not wanting to get verbally dressed down again. He couldn't recall a time when anybody talked to him like that. And what bothered him the most, wasn't what she said, or how she said it, but the fact she was right. He was always pushing her away, regardless of his feelings for her, and always seemed like he was giving her mixed signals. Maybe now he knew the CIA wasn't chasing after him anymore, he could have the life he once sought. The one he thought he would have with Carrie. The one Mia, at one time, wanted with him. It didn't seem likely at the moment he'd ever get a life with her now, seeing as how she had a boyfriend she appeared to be happy with. But maybe it was the missing piece inside him and why he always seemed drawn to her, even though he always convinced himself to leave. Maybe secretly he still yearned for that life, and until he fully admitted it to himself, he would never be free of the pain which always tormented him.

8
____

Recker tried calling Mia several times, though she never picked up. He wasn't sure of her work schedule these days, so it was possible she couldn't get to her phone. It was also equally possible she saw him calling and chose to ignore him. He sat down and put his elbows on his knees as he rubbed his eyes, not sure what to do next. Jones could see he was frustrated he couldn't get through to Mia and wondered what else was going through his mind. Though Recker wasn't showing any other outward signs of debate, Jones was sure he must've been having a lively conversation within himself, probably beating himself up over how he's handled things with her. Jones started to feel bad for his friend and tried to make things easier for him.

"Fine. I'll call her," Jones said.

"Well if she picks up right away I guess we'll know what's what."

Jones took out his phone and dialed Mia's number. Much to his surprise, she picked up barely after the second ring. It wasn't too surprising to Recker, however, as it merely confirmed what he suspected. She was in fact ignoring him.

"Mia. Hi."

"David. Hi," Mia said, mimicking his tone.

Jones coughed, trying to figure out the best way to begin. "So, um…"

Mia could tell right away by Jones' stammering he was uncomfortable with whatever he had to say and attempted to snuff out what she suspected it might be. "David, if you're calling to plead Mike's case, please don't bother. I know he's tried to call me a couple times, but right now I'm just not interested in talking to him. I said everything I had to say back at the hospital and nothing's changed since then."

Jones cleared his throat as he attempted to proceed. He might have been worse at relationships than Recker was. And he didn't even have a romantic interest in her. After all, telling someone their life is in danger isn't exactly a pleasant conversation.

"No, Mia, I'm not calling to talk about Michael."

"Then what? Is everything OK?" Mia asked, sounding concerned.

Though she had her issues with Recker at the moment, she didn't have those same problems with Jones. They'd always had a pleasant relationship, and probably because neither had romantic feelings for the other, always seemed to respect each other and their positions.

So if Jones was calling to discuss something other than her relationship with Recker, she knew something was amiss.

"What is it?" she asked again, knowing something was wrong.

"Well…"

"David, you always dance around the subject when you have bad news or you don't really wanna talk about what you need to talk about."

"I do?" Jones asked, not realizing he did.

"Yes. You do. Now spill it."

"Fine. The reason Mike's been calling you is not because he's trying to make up, well, he is, but it's not it right now."

"David," Mia said sternly.

"The reason we're both calling is, we're concerned for your safety right now," Jones said finally.

"My safety? What are you talking about? I'm fine."

"I only wish that was the case."

"David, just say it," Mia said, clearly getting worried.

"Several months ago, you and Mike were spotted in the hospital cafeteria by a very dangerous person who runs a rather large criminal enterprise in the city."

"And?"

"The man just gave Mike an ultimatum and is planning on using you for leverage," Jones said.

"Leverage? How? What would he want with me?"

"He doesn't want you per se. He wants Mike to kill Vincent for him so he can take control of the criminal enterprise of the city."

"I still don't get what this has to do with me."

"Because Mike doesn't want to do it."

"You mean there's someone out there Mike doesn't want to kill?" she asked sarcastically.

"Mia."

"I know. I'm sorry. Unfair."

"It's OK. Anyway, that's the gist of it, so we need you to lay low for a few days until we get things sorted out."

"Wait, wait, wait, wait, wait. That's it? There's gotta be more to it. What you told me doesn't seem to have anything to do with my laying low. Why would I have to do that? What are you not telling me?"

Jones sighed, knowing she was too smart to pull the wool over her eyes. "As I said, Mike doesn't want to kill Vincent, certainly not for someone else. This man, Jeremiah, has threatened to hurt you if Mike doesn't do it though."

"Why? What do I have to do with it?"

"Because he knows you're important to Mike, and he needs to use you as leverage to get Mike to do what he needs him to do."

"Yeah, well, if this guy really knew us he'd know I'm not important to him," Mia said.

"Mia, you know that's not the case."

"I'm not gonna hide somewhere, David. Just tell Mike to take care of it."

"It's not quite so simple."

Mia sighed loudly into the phone, fearing there was yet another shoe to drop. "Is there something else you're not saying?"

"Well, that's pretty much it," Jones said.

"David, if you don't spit out the rest of it, all of it, I'm hanging up this phone right now and never talking to either one of you again."

"Jeremiah's got men watching your every move."

"What?"

"If Mike doesn't kill Vincent within the week, then Jeremiah will have you dealt with."

"Dealt with? Are you trying to say he's planning on killing me?"

"Well, I was trying to say it a little more diplomatically, but that's basically the gist of it."

"Why do these things keep happening to me? You may not believe this but I never had my life threatened before I met you guys. Seems to be an annual occurrence now."

"I know. I'm sorry. I wish there was something else I could say."

"So what are we gonna do?" Mia asked.

"Until Jeremiah's been dealt with, we're going to have to keep you here for your safety."

"Here? Where? You mean your office?" she asked, clearly surprised.

"Unfortunately, yes. It's the safest place we know. We can't take you somewhere else and fight this threat effectively, so here it is."

Knowing there was nothing else to say and no use in fighting it, Mia resigned herself to her fate. At least for the moment. "So, should I just come there now or what? How are we doing this?"

"No. As I said, there are men watching you wherever you are. Where are you at right now?"

"At home."

"In order to bring you here safely, Mike's going to have to deal with the men watching you."

"Can't you just do it?"

"Mia, I understand your feelings right now, but for the moment, let's put all that aside for the betterment of the situation."

"OK. You're right. When's he gonna get here?"

"Good question. Uh, hold on, I'll get right back to you."

"You mean you haven't figured it out yet?"

"Well, no. We figured the toughest part was you agreeing to come with us," Jones said. "Let me talk to Mike and come up with a game plan and I'll call you right back."

Jones put the phone on the desk and turned toward Recker, wondering what their next move would be. Getting Mia on board was the first step, now, they had to figure out how to lose her watch dogs. Or kill them. Whichever would be easier.

"Well, we've got her in the loop, now how are we going to bring her in?" Jones said. "It's a cinch you can't just go over to her apartment, put her in the car, and drive over here."

"I'll have to meet her somewhere. A neutral location."

"Hospital's too dangerous," Jones said.

"Somewhere they haven't seen her go before, but a place we both know," Recker said, thinking of a location.

"Somewhere I can take out whoever's behind her without a crowd or alerting anyone who's nearby."

"Sounds like Jeremiah's meeting house."

"Yeah, someplace like that," Recker said, still thinking. "Wait. I've got it."

"Where?"

"Haddix Apartments. She knows it, I know it, and they've never seen her go there. If I get there first, I can see how many people follow her in."

"And if any shooting starts?"

"They'll be used to it. And it's not if... it's when. We'll do it tonight, use the cloak of darkness so we're not easily spotted by anyone."

Though they'd continue talking it over and come up with the exact specifics later, Jones called Mia back to let her know the general plan. She expressed disdain at going back to the Haddix Apartments after the last time she went there, but she reluctantly agreed to do it. She was told Recker would call her later with a more detailed plan, but for now just to stay put and get some time off from the hospital since they didn't know how long she'd be gone. With things settled for the time being, Jones would leave Recker to figure out how he was gonna save Mia. His chore was to get back to Bernal and find him.

Even though Jones was knee deep in trying to locate their target, and was a little behind due to the Mia situation, he still found some time to start running a new program. It was actually something Recker said to him before they left for Detroit, but it had been ruminating inside his head for a while as he considered the merits of it. Over the past year, they'd increasingly seen tougher and more dangerous assignments, and at times seemed like they had more work than they could handle. Now, Jones was finally ready to bring someone else aboard, if he could find someone who met his qualifications. Someone like Recker would be ideal, with his values, with his work ethic, with his skills, but maybe with slightly fewer violent tendencies. Jones didn't particularly care if it was a man or a woman, as long as they had the required prerequisites. It wasn't something he was ready to pour himself into totally yet, not with the other issues they had at the moment, but he could at least get the algorithms working.

When he ran his first program, it took Jones several months until he found Recker. He assumed if he constructed his software in a similar manner, the results would probably take around the same amount of time. Of course, with the experience of the first search, he could eliminate a few mistakes he made previously. He hadn't yet let Recker know he really was considering bringing someone new into the fold. He figured he would do that once the Mia situation was resolved and Bernal had been taken down. Since Recker was the one who originally mentioned it, Jones assumed he'd be relieved he was commencing the search. With Recker's input, it might even take less time than he anticipated, but it was something to worry about for another day. His chief concern at the moment was just bypassing the CIA's infrastructure without being noticed, which was no small task. Once he did that, he could start extracting the desired information a little at a time.

Recker saw Jones was feverishly working on the computer, splitting his time between several at once, though he didn't question what his partner was doing. He just assumed it was all in the effort of finding Bernal. But his main worry at the moment was protecting Mia. For the next several hours he went over various plans and ideas, tweaking a few things, abandoning other components entirely until he finally came up with something he was comfortable with. And something he legitimately thought would work. With Jones wrapped up in his own work, Recker didn't bother to share the details. All Jones needed to know was if it would work. Hopefully, it would. Any more issues might be too much for them to handle.

As the sun was setting, Recker grabbed his gear and left the office, only letting Jones know he'd be back later, with Mia of course. His plan was to survey the area of the Haddix Apartments, and even though he was already remotely familiar with it, he still preferred to stake it out for a while first to cement his getaway plan, just in case the police came in hot and heavy. Once he pulled into the parking lot of the apartments, he gave Mia a call to inform her of his plans. Though he was relatively sure she was going to answer his call this time, there was still part of him expecting a hostile response. Much to his surprise, the phone never got to a second ring.

"Hey," Mia said solemnly.

"Hey. So, I'm at the Haddix Apartments now. At eleven

o'clock, I want you to leave your place and head over here."

"Why do I have to wait so long? Why can't I just come over now?"

"It's gonna take me a little time to set some things up," Recker said.

"Set what up?"

"Well, I can't say yet. I wanna make sure it's viable first."

"OK."

Recker could hear in her voice that she seemed depressed and sought to reassure her. "Don't worry, I won't let anything happen to you."

"I know. I trust you completely," Mia said. "If there was anybody I had to do this with, you'd be the person I'd call."

"I guess this is the one thing I'm good at."

"Not the only thing."

"Yeah, well, I guess I'll see you when you get here."

"Wait. What do you want me to do when I arrive?"

"Go inside. When I figure out which apartment, I'll text you the number."

Recker went inside, and as Detective Scarborough, knocked on a few doors until he came across an empty apartment. It was just what he was looking for. He jimmied the lock of the apartment he was intending to use and looked around inside, just to make sure there would be no surprises later. Satisfied it would suit his purposes just fine, he texted the number to Mia. Then he went back outside to his car and drove out of the lot. Next to the apartments was a shopping center which Recker drove into and parked. The shopping center and apartments were separated by grass and a clumping of trees and bushes. There was a dirt path which led from the apartments to the center, but it was further down from where Recker was setting up. The foliage was thick and would allow Recker to stand beside the trees without being spotted from either the shopping center or the apartments. He could stay there and watch anybody coming into the apartments. Besides the trees and bushes, the spot he was standing was not well lit and nobody would be able to see him unless they already knew he was there, and even then it would be a stretch.

Recker was eager to see how many people would be following Mia. He estimated it would be three, though he had nothing to base that off of and was just a guess. He hoped it would be less since it would be less work for him. His plan was to pick off her guards, hopefully by splitting them up if possible. He didn't want Mia to get caught up in any crossfire, which is why he hoped to kill everyone before they knew he was there. As he waited amongst the trees and bushes for all the players to arrive, he mentally went over how he envisioned the events playing out. He also predicted any problems and how he would handle them if they arose.

As eleven o'clock hit, Recker noticed Mia's car pull in, right on time. He watched as she parked the car, then got out and entered the apartments. As directed, she went right to apartment 108. Recker left the door unlocked so she could go right in and wait for him. She felt uneasy being there, especially after what happened the last time she visited the place. It didn't help matters that it was so late at night. It was bad enough being there in the daytime, the night just made it seem worse. She also didn't like waiting in the apartment alone. But when Recker texted her the apartment number, he also gave her advance warning she'd be in there by herself for a few minutes until he arrived. It didn't really help her anxiety though.

Recker didn't especially like Mia being in the apartment by herself either, but he needed to see who was following her. About a minute after she arrived, a black SUV pulled into the lot. The vehicle stopped by the curb near the entrance and two rough looking characters got out of the back seat of the car and headed inside. Then the truck pulled into a parking spot, the driver staying inside and waiting for his friends to return. Though the rear of the truck was now facing Recker, he noticed as it pulled in there was also someone in the passenger side of the front seat. He emerged from the darkness of the trees and headed straight for the truck. He removed his police badge from his pocket and held it in his left hand, then gripped his gun in his right. His biggest fear then, was one of the men inside the car recognizing him and jumping out of the vehicle blasting away at him. After a minute of cautiously walking toward the car, Recker reached it without incident. He walked up to the driver side window and tapped on the glass, surprising the men inside. Recker showed his badge, and the driver sighed, thinking their plans had just gone down the drain, and reluctantly rolled down the window.

"What are you guys doing here tonight?" Recker asked.

"Nothing. Just waiting for a friend to come out."

"You guys carrying guns or anything?"

"No, sir."

"You guys work for Jeremiah, don't you?" Recker asked, ready to come up firing.

The two men inside the car looked at each other, wondering how he knew, and whether they should reveal the truth. The man in the passenger seat leaned forward and looked more closely at the man outside their window and thought he looked familiar. Before Jeremiah met with Recker to reveal his plans for Mia and Vincent, he had distributed Recker's picture to most of his men so they could be sure what he looked like in case they ran into him. The man in the car remembered the photo as he looked at the police officer questioning them.

"Wait a minute," the man said, squinting his eyes. "You're not a cop, are you? You're The Silencer."

Recker smiled. "You got me."

Recker immediately showed his gun and fired at the man in the passenger seat, hitting him three times in the chest. The driver reached for his gun but it was too late. By the time he put his hand on it, Recker had already hit him three times as well. Both men were killed instantly and Recker pushed the driver on his side across the middle console to prevent someone from seeing the dead man from a distance through the window. With those men taken care of, Recker turned around to head into the apartments. As he walked toward it, he reloaded his weapon in anticipation of the next round of action. Since the men inside the apartment didn't know what room Mia was in, Recker figured he'd run into them roaming around the hallways.

As soon as Recker entered the building, he saw one of them standing near the door, probably waiting for Mia to come out. The two men locked eyes and Recker instantly withdrew his gun and fired several shots at the unsuspecting man. Jeremiah's man was leaning against the wall, but slumped down to the ground as he held his midsection once the bullets entered his body. His shirt was soaked in blood as life quickly left his body. There was one man left. Recker didn't immediately see him and stood there silently, hoping to hear something to indicate where he was. Whether it was doors quickly opening and closing, or fast walking footsteps, anything that would give an indication of where the man was. Recker didn't hear anything though. Instead of standing there, or walking through the building to find the man, Recker instead went to room 108, just in the unlikely chance the man found where Mia was. Recker slowly opened the door and took a quick peek inside. He didn't see anybody at first glance. He stepped inside and closed the door behind him, still holding his gun, though he had it down by his leg.

"Mia," Recker whispered.

"Mike?" Mia asked, though Recker still couldn't see her.

Mia emerged from the kitchen where she'd been hiding. It wasn't much of a hiding spot, but in the event someone other than Recker came in, she didn't want to be standing in the middle of the room out in the open. She was relieved to see that it was him. She wasn't ecstatic to be there to begin with, but being there by herself in a strange room, in the middle of the night, had her terrified. Even though she knew Recker was in the vicinity, unlike the last time she was there, her nerves were still a wreck. Upon seeing him, Mia ran up to him and wrapped her arms around him, giving him a big hug.

"I'm so glad you're here," she said, holding him tight. "I'm not cut out for this type of stuff."

"Most people aren't," he said, enjoying holding her once again.

"I've been so scared waiting in here, thinking someone unpleasant was going to come in."

"I know. It's almost over."

"Almost? It's not done yet?" Mia asked, looking worried, as they released each other from their embrace.

"There were four men watching you. I've already taken out three."

"When you say taken out, you mean…"

"Killed. I told you I'd always protect you. No matter what you think of me."

"So, what about the last one?"

"I'll take care of him."

"How?"

"Well, he's somewhere inside the building. Probably

checking the other floors. But he'll have to come out front at some point," Recker said.

Recker quickly tried to formulate a plan which wouldn't put Mia in any danger. Without knowing exactly where the other man was made things more difficult. There was a staircase at each end of the hall leading up to the higher floors, not to mention an elevator toward the middle of the building. It meant Recker couldn't stake out one spot, fearing the man could come out via another alternative.

"Why can't we just go now?" Mia asked. "Forget about the other guy."

"What if we start leaving and he sees us as we go out the door and pursues us? Or what if he sees us and don't know he's there and he takes a shot and hits one of us?"

"I just want this to be over."

"I know. And it will be… soon," Recker said.

The other thing complicating the situation for Recker was sure he'd be recognized as soon as the man saw him. Seeing as how Jeremiah's man in the car knew who he was, albeit a little late, it was a sign that Recker's picture had been distributed among the gang leader's men. Recker thought about just staying in the apartment with the door ajar slightly, so he could see anyone passing by, but there was a possibility the man might not come that way if he chose the elevator or other staircase. As he thought about how to move forward, Mia asked him what he was thinking, and Recker relayed the concerns running through his mind.

"Fine. Use me as bait," she said.

"What?" Recker asked, surprised at the request.

"Use me as bait."

"I'm not doing that."

"Mike, I trust you completely. I know you won't let anything happen to me. It doesn't mean I won't be scared out of my mind, but I know you'll protect me. You always have."

"I dunno."

"It's the best way, right?"

"I don't know. Maybe," Recker said, still not sold on the idea.

"Hurry up before I lose my nerve."

Recker sighed and looked away, not really wanting to agree to the plan, but not having any better options either.

"Would you do it if it was someone other than me?" Mia asked.

"Probably."

"Then treat me as if I was anybody else."

Recker nodded, reluctantly agreeing to her proposition. "But you're not anybody else."

She gave him a nervous smile as she waited for instructions. "So, what do you want me to do?"

"Well, seeing as it is you, I want you within arm's reach of me if something goes wrong," Recker said. "Stand just outside the door and keep your hand on the knob. You keep watching both directions, and as soon as you see someone coming, you duck inside. We'll keep the door open so it looks like you're just coming in."

"OK. What are you gonna do?"

"Well as soon as he sees it's you he's gonna follow you

and see what number you ducked into. As soon I get sight of him, I'll start firing."

"This will work, right?" Mia asked nervously.

"It'll work. Promise."

Even though Mia had issues with Recker about how he viewed and handled their personal relationship, there was no doubt in her mind, nobody would be better to handle their current predicament than him. There was something soothing in his voice when he confidently said he'd handle something. Though there were never guarantees with anything, especially in volatile situations involving men with guns, but Recker's word was as close to one as humanly possible. Before she lost her nerve, Mia went over to the door and opened it, though Recker stopped her before she went into the hall. Recker wanted to make sure she didn't run into a surprise out there and stuck his head out the door first. With the coast clear, he signaled that she was good to go.

"How long do you think this will take?" Mia said.

"Not long. He should be here within a few minutes."

"What if he's already been by here and just goes outside instead?"

"Then he'll find his buddies and make his way back inside to find the person who did it," Recker said. "Either way, he'll be along soon. Remember, as soon as you see him, don't waste any time in getting in here."

"I'll remember."

Recker initially had thoughts about having her wait by the elevator. He could have probably covered her from the same door he was in, but he thought it was too risky. It was a longer shot to take, and he'd also risk the man taking Mia as hostage if Recker missed his first shot. In the end, Recker figured this was a much easier and less risky plan which didn't involve putting Mia in as much danger. He knew the man wouldn't come up shooting at Mia since Jeremiah needed her alive to keep Recker in line. Just as Recker suggested, it didn't take long to put the plan in action. Within three minutes of her standing in the hall, the man came pouncing down the stairs and threw open the door as he walked into the hallway. Mia immediately saw him enter and waited a split second until she was sure that the man locked eyes on her. As soon as he did, she pushed open the door and went into the apartment.

"He's coming," she said.

"Go in the kitchen and wait," Recker said. "Which way's he coming from."

"Your right."

Recker stood behind the door, still leaving it open a crack. He looked through the peephole until he saw the man approaching the door. The man cautiously approached the apartment and saw the door was not fully closed. He took a few steps toward the door and put his right hand on the front of his pants, presumably reaching for a weapon. Recker wasn't going to give him a chance to use it though. He violently flung the door open and stepped into the frame of the door in full view of the unsuspecting man. The dark-haired man tried to withdraw his gun from his pants but Recker was too quick for him. Recker started shooting, hitting the man in the chest and stomach at point blank range, continuing to fire until the man dropped to the ground. After the fifth bullet entered the man's body, Recker stopped the carnage and went into the hallway, looking around for onlookers. He quickly picked up the man's gun and grabbed his feet, dragging him into the apartment before the curious crowd showed up.

One of the perks of picking the Haddix building was the residents were used to gunfire, hearing it fairly frequently. Any other building probably would've brought out the apartment dwellers almost immediately. Here, though, most people weren't too keen on popping their head out of their door too quickly, for fear of catching a bullet after the fact. Plus, not very many people were very interested in being witnesses. The residents of the Haddix building mostly just wanted to be left alone and minded their own business. As Recker dragged the man's lifeless body into the living room, Mia showed herself from the kitchen, observing him leave the dead body as he went back to the door.

"All right, coast is clear," Recker said. "We've gotta hurry before the police show up."

Recker grabbed Mia's hand and led her down the hallway, leaving the building via a side exit located by the stairways at the end of the hall. As Recker led her away from the apartment building and through the trees and bushes on the side of the property, Mia was confused at where they were going.

"Where's your car? Where are we going?" she asked.

"This leads to the shopping center on the other side. My car's over there."

"Why?"

"That way nobody would see us leaving," Recker said. "Or if the police came before we left, we wouldn't have issues getting out of here."

"Oh."

Within minutes they were on the other side of the divider, quickly scurrying to Recker's car, though Mia was concerned about the fate of her own vehicle.

"What about my car?"

"We'll have to leave it for now," Recker said.

"Why couldn't I just follow you?"

"Because we can't risk it. Once Jeremiah realizes what happened, he'll put an alert out on your car. Every man he's got will be all over the city looking for it. And when they find it, they'll know where you are."

"I guess that makes sense. But doesn't he know your car? Won't he come looking for that instead?"

"Except I put on a different license plate every time I see him, just in case he's tagged it. That way I avoid that problem."

"Sounds like an awful lot of work," Mia said.

"Not as much work as doing this."

9

———

Just to make sure they weren't followed, Recker drove around for an extra thirty minutes, paying careful attention to any cars behind him. It would have had to be an excellent tail job to be able to follow him based on the circumstances, and since Recker was a master at this type of work. He hadn't met a tail yet he wasn't able to get rid of. Luckily, there was nothing he had to shake this night. When he pulled into the parking lot of the office shopping center, Mia was still confused at what they were doing.

"I thought we were going to the office," Mia said.

"We are."

"Uh, there's no offices here. Are there?"

Recker smiled. "The laundromat."

"Seriously?"

"What?"

"You two are running your entire operation out of a laundromat?"

"Of course not. There's an office over the top of it."

"Oh. Makes perfect sense," she said with an eye roll.

Recker led her around the back of the building and up the wooden steps to the office door. He could tell Jones was still awake since all the lights were still on.

"Home sweet home," Recker said, unlocking the door.

As they came into the office, Jones got up from his chair and walked over to the middle of the room to greet them. Seeing someone new come into their sanctuary was a nerve-wracking experience, even though it was a person they both knew well. It was still a day Jones had never anticipated having.

"Glad to see you both made it in one piece," Jones said, scanning the both of them for holes. "You are both in one piece, aren't you?"

"As far as we know," Recker said, patting his chest.

"Hi David," Mia said.

Jones gave her a smile, happy to see her in surprisingly good spirits. At least outwardly anyway. She didn't appear to be harmed or injured in any way, and her face didn't look all doom and gloom. But she stood by the door for a minute, like she was afraid or nervous to come in any further. Jones went over to her and gave her a hug, then took her arm to try to make her more comfortable.

"Wasn't sure if you'd still be awake," Recker said.

"You really thought I'd go to sleep before you came back or before I knew you escaped unharmed?" Jones asked.

"You really thought I might have problems?"

"Even you, Michael, can run into something you're not prepared to handle."

"So, this is where everything happens, huh?" Mia asked, looking around the room.

"This is it," Jones said.

"It's not quite what I expected," Mia said.

"It grows on you," Recker said.

"What were you expecting?" Jones asked.

"I don't know. Something a little fancier I guess."

"You mean marble floors, crystal chandeliers, tons of windows, things like that?"

"Uh, yeah, I guess."

Jones smiled, amused as he looked around the room himself. "Yes, it's not quite the Hilton, is it? But it works well and suits our purposes."

"Over a laundromat... not at all what I was expecting."

"All the five floor office buildings were taken," Recker said sarcastically.

"Don't you ever get any prying eyes or anything?" she asked.

"No. This is actually a perfect setup for us," Jones said.

"Am I the first person to ever be in here with you guys?"

"You're the first."

"I guess I should be honored you think so highly of me to allow me to be here," Mia said sheepishly.

"Did you bring some luggage or a bag of your things or anything?" Jones asked.

"Uh, well, I did. But I left the bag in my car. I didn't

realize I'd be leaving it there."

"You left her car?"

"Figured it'd be better that way," Recker said. "If Jeremiah goes out looking for it, I didn't want it to be parked here. This way, he's got no way of knowing where she went."

Jones nodded, approving of his plan. "Good idea."

Mia walked over to the couch and plopped down in the middle of it, sizing it up. "Guess I'm sleeping on here tonight?"

"I'm sorry," Jones said. "It is quite comfortable though, I've spent many a night on there myself."

"It'll be fine," she said, faking a smile.

Jones told her where the bathroom was if she needed to use it, or if she wanted to take a shower in the morning. He also pointed out the Keurig machine, as well as the refrigerator, which was pretty well stocked with food at the moment, and told her to help herself to anything she wanted.

"What am I gonna do for clothes and necessities?" Mia said.

Recker and Jones looked dumbfounded as they stared at each other, neither of whom had thought much about her request prior to that.

"Drive back to her car and get her bag?" Jones asked. "Or stop by her apartment and grab a few things?"

"No, too risky for that," Recker said. "Just in case Jeremiah keeps a man on her car or her apartment in the event she comes back."

"I guess one of us can go to the store and pick out

some things for her for the morning."

"One of us?"

"Well we certainly can't take her and parade her around in the store, can we?" Jones asked.

"I suppose not."

"You guys are gonna stay here tonight with me, right?" Mia asked. "I really don't wanna stay here by myself."

"Of course," Jones said, smiling, trying to put her mind at ease. "One of us often stays here, anyway. That's why there are two couches."

"So what are we gonna do?" Recker whispered in Jones' ear.

"Well, I suppose one of us stays here tonight and the other can go to the store and pick up what she needs."

"So who's doing what?"

"Well, considering your history with her, do you think it's wise if you stayed the night?"

Recker took a good long look at Mia and carefully considered the question, thinking about her attitude toward him lately, notwithstanding at the apartment, and also thinking about her current boyfriend. "No, I guess not."

"So I'll stay the night with her," Jones said. "Why don't you go to the store and pick up things she needs and come back in the morning with them?"

"What kind of things?"

"I don't know. Clothes and necessities are what she said."

"What kind of necessities?" Recker asked, fearful of what they might entail.

"I suppose we should ask her." Jones shrugged, turning back to their guest. "Mia, what exactly do you need?"

"Well how long do you think I'll be staying here?"

"A few days I suspect. A week at the most I would think."

"Pants, socks, a few shirts," she said. "You've seen the things I wear. You know what I like."

"I guess I can handle that," Recker said.

"I guess I also need a toothbrush, bras, and underwear," Mia said, not thinking much about it.

Recker, on the other hand, was not as comfortable with the request. He looked at Jones who was looking back at him just as uncomfortably, the professor glad he wasn't the one heading to the store to fulfill her shopping list.

"Uh... I'm not so sure I can handle that," Recker said.

"It's just clothes," Jones said nonchalantly, trying not to make a big deal of it.

"David, it's bras and underwear. I'm not equipped for that."

"Nonsense. Don't even think about it."

"Guns. I like guns. I'm familiar with guns. I know about guns. I can handle guns. I don't know about bras and underwear."

"Do you mean to tell me you can shoot five men point blank standing in front of you without a second thought and you're going to stand here freaking out about underwear?" Jones asked.

"Women's underwear. It means I have to go... look at

them... touch them.”

“You certainly have some strange views on things.”

“How do I know what fits?”

“Umm...,” Jones said, struggling to come up with an answer.

Seeing and overhearing Recker and Jones’ conversation, Mia couldn’t help but let out a laugh and shake her head at them. She thought it amusing how men like them, especially Recker, could have fears about picking out a lady’s undergarments. After thinking about it for a minute, though, she figured it was understandable. It wasn’t exactly their usual cup of tea.

“Would it be helpful if I wrote down my sizes?” Mia asked.

“Uh.” Recker was lost for words, looking at Jones. “Yes?”

Mia smiled again. “Get me a piece of paper and pen and I’ll write down what I need. I’ll make it extremely easy for you.”

Jones did as she asked and supplied her with a pen and paper. She immediately wrote down the items that she needed then walked over to Recker and handed it to him. She could see the fear was still ingrained in his face as he thought about getting the items.

“It’s really not that bad,” Mia said, trying to ease his fears. “Nobody will look at you funny for buying ladies bras and underwear. Men do it all the time.”

“They do?” Recker asked.

“Sure. We’re in the twenty-first century now, remember?”

"Oh. Well can't you just go without, um," Recker said, looking briefly at her chest. "Uh, no, never mind, I guess not."

Jones had sat back down at one of the computer terminals and put his hand over his mouth to prevent himself from laughing or smiling. He sympathized with Recker's fears as he wouldn't have been too keen on going to the store to pick up her things either. He was glad he chose to stay the night and convinced him it was the best option. Mia went into the bathroom for a minute to get ready for bed. While she was in there, Recker tried one last time to switch jobs.

"You sure you wouldn't rather change things?" Recker asked. "I mean, I'm out there far more than you are. It'd probably be good for you to get out for a little while. Smell the air."

"No, I'm quite content staying here for the night. Besides, I'm more used to staying the night here than you are."

"Oh. OK."

As soon as Mia came out of the bathroom, she went straight for Recker. He was standing near the door and ready to go. He just wanted to say goodnight to her before he left. She had a few things on her mind she wanted to talk to him about. Things that had been bothering her since their last conversation at the hospital. She looked at the floor, unsure where to begin.

"I guess, um, I need to apologize," Mia said.

"For?"

"You know, the things I told you in the cafeteria the

other day."

Recker shook his head. "Mia, you don't have to do anything. It's fine. I'm not mad. I'm not upset. You had a right to say what you felt. It's no big deal. Apologies aren't necessary."

"No, they are. For me they are. In truth, I'm happy you're back."

"You are?"

Mia nodded, looking down again. "I was just hurt that you dropped off the grid like that. Especially at a time when I could've used a friend."

Recker squeezed his eyebrows together, unsure what she was referring to. "What are you talking about? Are you OK?"

"Yeah, pretty much. Remember you asked how things were with me and Josh?"

"Yeah. I think you said everything was fine."

"Yeah, I lied," she said, forcing a smile. "We, uh, broke up a couple months after you left. I think it was actually the week before I lost contact with you."

Recker looked away from her and glared at the wall, mad at himself for abandoning her. "I'm sorry."

"It's OK."

"Why didn't you say something the other day?" Recker said.

"I don't know. I guess I was just scared. I didn't want to admit how much pain I was in. And I guess when I saw you sitting there, it made me realize how much I actually missed you while you were gone. I guess it's why I snapped at you the way I did."

"He didn't... hurt you or anything, did he?"

"No, no, nothing like that. We just wanted different things. He was more interested in work and moving up the ladder. He's ambitious. And I'm just at the point where I want something more."

"Why didn't you tell me before?"

"I guess I didn't know what to say. I mean, what would you have done? Move back just to console my broken heart?"

"I dunno." Recker sighed. "Maybe I would've done things differently."

"You mean not dropped off the planet for three months?" Mia asked with a smile.

"Yeah, maybe."

"What I said, about leaving is what you know how to do best... I didn't mean it. It was someone else talking."

"No, it was you. It's probably something you've been wanting to say for a while, you just buried it down deep," Recker said. "The pain you were in just made it easier for it to come out."

"Maybe. Anyway, I hope you forgive me."

"Mia, there's nothing to forgive. I wasn't mad at you for what you said. In fact, most of it I probably agreed with."

"Do you think we can get back to the way we were before?" Mia asked, hoping to resume their friendship.

"I would like that."

Recker had serious thoughts about telling her he'd like to be more, but decided it wasn't the best time to drop news like that on her. Though he did miss Philadelphia while he was gone, and it really was like home to him, he realized what he missed most about the city was her. The memory of her soft green eyes, her silky black hair, her pretty face, remembering what her touch felt like, that's what kept drawing him back. Now the CIA wasn't on his tail, he began thinking maybe it was possible to do what he wanted to do with Carrie several years ago. He could actually move on. But those were thoughts he figured were better left to himself, at least for the time being. Maybe when the situation with Jeremiah was over, and they figured out where Bernal was, then he could figure out exactly what he wanted and with whom.

"Are you going to be OK with work?" Recker asked.

"Yeah, I'll be fine. I told them yesterday I had a family emergency, and I'd be away for a week."

"You're not going to get in trouble or anything?"

"No. I have five sick days I can use," Mia said. "If I need more, then I can use some of my vacation days. So, don't worry, everything's fine."

"Now I think of it, I guess it explains why you didn't put up any kind of a fight about leaving your boyfriend."

Mia let out a smile, "yeah, no use in fighting about leaving a boyfriend you don't have."

"Well, I should be going," Recker said. "You need anything?"

"Umm, a hug would be nice."

It was a request Recker couldn't, and wouldn't, deny. For the first time, his thoughts weren't to resist or hold back. He eagerly took her in his arms and tightly wrapped them around her as she embraced their closeness. She buried her head into his chest as she relished the affection he was showing. A few tears rolled down her face as she thought about the trouble she was in. Up until then, she'd put on a brave face and tried not to think about it too much. But she was only human, and a life of danger wasn't exactly something she was used to, or signed up for. She was usually a pretty strong person, but being targeted by a violent criminal gang was hard to deal with, even though she had someone like Recker looking after her. Recker could hear her sniffling and felt bad she had to go through this.

"It'll be over soon," he said softly.

Unlike previous times they'd embraced, Recker was in no hurry to let it end. He wasn't trying to pull back, or worrying about giving her false hope, or trying to convince himself it was a bad idea. He was just living in the moment. When they first began hugging, Jones looked away and started typing away on the computer, trying to keep himself busy during their moment of affection. He periodically looked back at them to see if they'd disengaged, but he was quite surprised to see how long their embrace was lasting. As Jones watched them, he figured it was the type of embrace which was probably a couple years overdue. For some time now, Jones assumed eventually the two of them would get to this point. They had a brief lapse of affection after he rescued her at the cemetery, but as they always did, managed to pull themselves apart after deciding it wasn't the right thing to do.

For Recker's sake, Jones hoped this time they had found each other for good. Even though in the beginning, Jones didn't think it was wise for him to get involved with

Mia, or anybody else, he'd begun to realize Recker needed something else in his life. Maybe it was to replace the feeling of emptiness from losing Carrie, or maybe because Recker always seemed to long for something else, something to justify himself other than simply being known as a killer. With the CIA no longer following him, with Agent 17 no longer on his mind, Jones thought the time was finally right for Recker to lose the binds that tied up his soul. After a few more minutes, Recker and Mia finally were able to tear themselves away from each other.

"Well, I should be going," Recker said.

Mia laughed, wiping her eyes. "Yeah, I think you said so already."

Recker put his hand on her face and stared into Mia's eyes as they got lost in each other's gaze. He wiped some of the tears away with his thumb. She brought her hand up to her face and put it on top of his hand, gently rubbing his skin as she basked at his touch.

"When this is over, things will be different," Recker said. "For us."

Mia looked at him in amazement, not believing what just came out of his mouth. For so long she'd waited and hoped for him to say that he wanted her. It wasn't quite riding the white horse and sweeping her off her feet, but it was probably as close as he'd ever get. A smile came over her face as she thought about the possibility of them finally being together.

"But—" Mia said before being interrupted.

"No more buts, or ifs, or maybe's. No more games

between us. I don't wanna deny what I feel for you anymore."

Tears started forming in Mia's eyes again as she realized what he was saying. Now she just had to hope he wasn't delirious or losing his mind in the excitement of the situation. Or that a good night's sleep wouldn't change his mind when he saw her again in the morning. On most nights, the implication of them being together would be enough to keep her up for hours in lieu of sleep, but with everything that had happened so far, even this news wouldn't cure her exhaustion.

"Get some sleep," Recker said, kissing her forehead. "I'll see you in the morning."

Once Recker left the office, Mia did an about face and turned toward Jones. "Did that just happen?" she asked, worried maybe she was hallucinating.

"It just happened," Jones said.

"I mean, I'm not dreaming, or seeing things, or talking to people who aren't there or anything, am I?"

Jones laughed, finding amusement in her fears. "No. He was really there."

"Good, 'cause I really thought maybe I'd lost my mind there for a second. I mean, he actually seemed like he wanted me for a second."

"Isn't it what you want?"

"Yes. I just hope he wasn't saying it to make me feel better or something and that he meant it."

"Have you ever known Michael to say something he didn't mean?" Jones asked.

"No."

"Then I'm sure he did."

"Would you be OK with it?" Mia asked, sensing he wasn't overjoyed by the prospect of them being together.

"Why wouldn't I be?"

"Well, I don't know, I just remember you saying something along the lines of like this wasn't possible for us."

"Circumstances change," Jones said. "At one time, I did believe him getting into a relationship with you would've been a mistake."

"But not now?"

"Now he's free from the CIA, he's avenged Carrie's death, there's nothing holding him back anymore. I think ever since I met him, there was something missing inside him. I thought for the longest time, it was just the pain of losing Carrie eating away at him, and once he killed the man responsible, that would have cured it."

"But it didn't?"

"No. I think what he's been looking for has been fulfillment. To feel whole again. It's what he had with Carrie. He felt complete. It's what he's been looking for, what he's needed."

"But why did it take so long for him to see I was standing right in front of him?"

Jones smiled at her. "I think he's always known. He could have never done this if the CIA was still looking for him. Because he was a target, you would be a target, and he would never allow you to end up harmed because of him. But once he knew he was free from them, he finally realized what would make him whole again. And it was you."

10

———

By the time Recker showed up the following morning, both Jones and Mia were already awake. They'd showered and eaten something out of the fridge and were sitting at the table having some coffee when Recker walked in after ten.

"Thought maybe you'd forgotten about us," Mia said, smiling.

"Not likely," Recker said.

"A little later than usual," Jones said.

"Well I had to make pit stops," Recker said, holding up a shopping bag.

Recker walked over to the couch and plopped the bag on it as the others came over and joined him. He started to reach into the bag to take out what he'd bought but brought his hand back out of it as he thought better of it.

"Enjoy your trip?" Mia asked, a big smile on her face, enjoying watching Recker squirm.

"Yes, Mike, enjoy your trip?" Jones said, piling on.

"No and no, I did not enjoy my trip."

"Get everything?" Mia asked, looking into the bag.

"Everything you wrote down," Recker said.

"See, it wasn't so bad, was it?"

"It was terrifying."

"Really?" Mia asked, believing he was exaggerating.

"I was standing by the rack, looking at the, uh, the uh," Recker said, pointing at his chest. "The uh, you know."

"Bras?"

"Yeah, those. I know there were other women passing by giving me strange looks."

Mia laughed, amused at how traumatized he seemed to be. "I know it was hard for you, thank you," she said, giving Recker a hug. "I'll be back."

Mia took the bag into the bathroom to change as Recker and Jones watched her walk away. Once she closed the door, Recker could feel Jones' eyes beating down on him. He slowly moved his head and looked at his partner out of the corner of his eye.

"Can I help you?" Recker asked, turning his head fully.

"About last night."

"What about it?"

"Did you mean what you told her?" Jones asked.

"In regard to what? Were you eavesdropping?"

"It's not eavesdropping if you're talking loud enough for other people in the room to hear. And in regard to telling her things would be different between you."

"Fair point," Recker said. "And I did mean it. Every word."

"Why the sudden change of heart?"

"I don't know. I guess seeing her in danger just triggered something in me. It wasn't something I was planning on doing or saying. Seeing her crying on my shoulder, it just kind of came out. Think it was a mistake?"

"Not if it's what's in your heart."

"So, you approve?"

"I'm not your father or your keeper, Mike. If being with her makes you happy, if it's what makes you whole again, then you have my blessing. Not that you need it."

"It does it make it easier knowing you're on board with it."

"I do have one question, though," Jones said. "Would you be proceeding with her if Ms. Lawson hadn't put you in the clear?"

"Unlikely. I lost one before because of the CIA. I wouldn't risk another, even if it meant me being miserable for the rest of my life."

"I want you to know I'm not trying to talk you out of this, but it seems to me you have another problem if you and her co-mingle."

"What's that?"

"It occurs to me, even if the CIA isn't after you, she still may be in danger. Look at what's happening now. Because of what you do, and your relationship with her, she's still a target," Jones said.

"So, what should I do? Never have a life outside of killing people?"

"That's not what I said. You just need to be cautious. If

others with a similar mind to Jeremiah know of her... is all I'm saying."

"Once I get rid of Jeremiah, there will be no others," Recker said confidently.

"You're forgetting Vincent."

"I'm not forgetting him. I just don't think he'd ever stoop so low."

"You're putting a lot of faith in someone who is, let's just say, not on the side of the city," Jones said.

"He may not be. But I think, even at his lowest point, he still has some honor."

"Honor among thieves?"

"Something like that."

"And if he doesn't?" Jones asked.

"Then he'll fall like the others and I'll deal with it when the time comes."

Mia exited the bathroom, feeling refreshed from the change of clothes. She threw her arms out as if she was modeling her new wardrobe. She wasn't wearing anything fancy, just a t-shirt, jeans, and sneakers. But it fit nicely on her and was comfortable. Recker had good taste in women's clothes, she thought. She gave him a break and didn't tell him and tease him further.

"How do I look?" she asked.

"Great," Recker said.

"Well, with the pleasantries out of the way, I do believe it's time to get back to work," Jones said, sitting down at his computer. "In case anyone's forgotten, we do still have a cop hater on the loose."

"Oh, yeah, um, what do you want me to do?" Mia asked, drawing a look from both Recker and Jones.

"Do?" Jones asked.

"Yeah. I mean, I can help somehow," she said.

"Doing what?" Recker said.

"I dunno, beats me. But just point me in the right direction and let me do something."

"Mia, we have very complicated systems and software programs in place," Jones said.

"So, what do you want me to do? Just sit around and play solitaire all day and watch daytime soap operas while you two do all the work?"

Recker looked over at Jones and raised his eyebrows. "She's got a point."

"I'm not computer illiterate, you know," Mia said. "I may not be a wiz like you guys but I know how to move a mouse and type. You're looking for some guy, I can help. Four eyes are better than two."

"Fine," Jones said finally. "Pull up a chair."

Mia smiled and clapped her hands together as she rushed over to a chair and spun it around next to Jones. Though Recker was fairly good with computers himself, Jones was obviously the expert, and he'd be the one to show her what he needed and what she could do. As the day wore on, Mia actually handled herself pretty well and was more proficient than Jones assumed. Jones was impressed with what she was able to accomplish. She was no expert, but he didn't have to keep looking over her shoulder to make sure she was on task either. The situation with Bernal and Officer Perez was explained to her, and with Jones' guidance, they continued their search for the pardoned criminal.

While they were on the Bernal case, Recker started looking for ways to end the fight with Jeremiah. Though Recker had known the gang leader for several years, there was still so much Recker didn't know about him. Since they'd always had a good relationship, or at least cordial, and with all the other cases he had to work on, Recker never assembled as thorough a file on Jeremiah as he should have. Though he could try to pump Tyrell for more information, Recker wasn't sure how forthcoming he'd be. Both Recker and Jeremiah frequently paid Tyrell for his time and information on different projects, so it was unlikely he'd willingly offer to give up either of his payment distributors. Recker had heard of a few spots where Jeremiah liked to hang out or frequent over the years, but no place where he would definitely be at a specified time. Since Recker only met him at the boarded-up house for their meetings, and Jeremiah was unlikely to go back there until their business was concluded, he had to somehow figure out where he would be in order to take him out.

As the day grew longer, there didn't turn out to be much success on anybody's front. Recker exhausted his resources to find Jeremiah, but didn't get even one lead. He reached out to Tyrell as a last-ditch effort, but never got a return call from him. Jones and Mia also came up empty after trying to find Bernal. They tried everything they could think of, retraced their steps, but couldn't come up with a location. Seeing as it'd already been several days since they began their search, they assumed time was running short. Recker was ready to use desperate measures. He began pacing around the room, which was usually an indication to Jones that something was on his mind.

"I think it's time," Recker said.

"Time for what?" Jones asked.

"Time to get Vincent involved," Recker said as he stopped pacing to look at him. "I don't think we have another choice anymore."

"I thought you said you didn't want to get him involved?"

"I didn't. But what we're doing isn't working."

"Just to be clear, exactly which case are you interested in bringing him on board with?" Jones asked.

"Bernal."

"And why would he? What are we offering?"

"A deal," Recker said. "If he can find Bernal, I'll take out Jeremiah for him."

"What makes you think he'd agree?"

"You don't think he'd agree to a deal where his competition is eliminated?"

"Yes, I know it's enticing, but what makes us believe he can find Bernal either?"

"I don't know if he can," Recker said. "But it's more than we got now. How many more days can we go on with nothing?"

An agonized look came over Jones, knowing Recker was probably correct in his assessment. "I don't know. But

I do know Bernal is unlikely to wait much longer to extract his own justice."

Recker grabbed his phone and called Jimmy Malloy, the usual protocol for getting in touch with Vincent. Even though Recker had a direct line to the crime boss, unless it was an immediate emergency, Vincent preferred Malloy being the principal contact. Within ten minutes, Recker got a call back from Malloy, telling him Vincent was willing to meet with him in one hour at the usual restaurant.

"That was fast," Jones said.

"Well I did say as quick as possible."

Recker wanted to be as prepared as possible for the meeting and printed out all the information they had on Bernal, so he had something to show Vincent, in the event he was willing to help. After taking a few minutes to print everything out, Recker put it in a file folder and got ready to leave. He touched Mia on the shoulder and told Jones he'd be back immediately after the meeting unless something else came up.

Once Recker got to the diner, he saw the same guard as usual at the door. Instead of going through the usual song and dance over his guns, he decided to just leave them in the car, only carrying the file folder with him. As he approached the entrance, the guard put his hand up as if to stop him from going any further. Recker simply opened his coat so he could see he wasn't armed.

"Figured I'd save us both the hassle and left them in the car," Recker said.

The guard shrugged. "I was gonna tell you not to

worry about your guns today. You were getting a free pass."

"Are you serious?"

"Boss said you didn't need to be checked today. Guess you've graduated to trustworthy status."

"I should've graduated to sainthood status by now," Recker said, drawing a laugh from the guard. The guard opened the door for him, where he was immediately greeted by Malloy. "Don't you guys ever get tired of the same old thing?" Recker asked. "Maybe you should switch it up sometimes. Maybe every now and then have Vincent greet me at the door and you sit at the table."

Malloy grinned at the humor, though he didn't deem it worthy of a response. Instead, he did like he usually did, and led Recker to the back of the diner at the booth where Vincent was sitting. The boss was just about to cut into a steak dinner as Recker sat down across from him. Recker noticed he also had a plate in front of him.

"I took the liberty of ordering for you," Vincent said.

"Thanks."

"So, what do I owe the pleasure of this meeting?" Vincent chewed at his first forkful of steak, closing his eyes as he savored the flavor.

"Well, first, thanks for meeting me so soon. I was expecting to have to wait a little bit," Recker said.

"It's a good thing you contacted me before dinner."

"Anyway, I wanted to conduct some business with you."

"Oh?" Vincent asked, putting his fork in his mouth again.

"Well, first off, I have a few questions I'd like you to answer if you could."

"Depends what they are."

"Have you been having problems with Jeremiah lately?" Recker said.

"Problems? In what way?"

Recker shrugged. "In any way. Are you starting to jockey for position with him?"

Vincent put his fork down and sighed, pondering the question for a minute, and not looking too pleased at it even being presented. "In the past couple of months, I have transacted some business in what would be constituted as Jeremiah's territory. But it's not with the intent of beginning a war or playing any kind of game with him. I simply began doing some business with a new player and, much to my dismay, they only agreed to conduct it in Jeremiah's part of town."

"So, you're not actively trying to eliminate him?" Recker asked bluntly.

"Not at the present time. In another year or so, who knows? But right now, it's not on my plate so to speak. Why do you ask? Have you heard rumblings of a problem with him?"

Recker tilted his head and stretched his facial muscles, indicating he had. "Yeah, I guess you could say that."

"What have you heard?" Vincent asked.

"It goes a little deeper than just hearing a rumor."

"Considering I haven't heard anything, you seem to have me at a disadvantage."

"I actually had a meeting with Jeremiah yesterday," Recker said.

"I see," Vincent said, looking very concerned. "And the contents of the meeting."

"Largely you. He told me he thinks you're moving in on his territory and planning on eliminating him. He wants to hit you first before you get him."

"Hmm. That's an unfortunate turn of events," Vincent said, wiping his mouth with a napkin. "I appreciate you coming to me with this."

"There's more," Recker said.

"OK?"

"He wants me to kill you."

For the first time since Recker had known Vincent, he actually looked a little nervous. Sitting there across from him, seeing firsthand what Recker was capable of, knowing how dangerous he was, Vincent was worried about the revelation.

"And your reply?" Vincent asked.

"I'm not interested."

"Well I must say it's a relief to hear that, but why?"

"Because I have no quarrel with you," Recker said. "You and I have done business nicely together up until now. I've done things for you, you've done things for me. I see no reason why the situation can't continue."

"I would tend to agree," Vincent said, nodding. "I'll owe you for this."

"Don't mention it."

"I'll have to be cautious in the coming weeks and months."

"It actually brings me to why I'm here. I told you I had some business for you."

"That wasn't it?"

"No. There's more," Recker said.

"I'm listening."

"I'm willing to take Jeremiah out for you if you do me a favor."

"And the favor is?"

Recker slid the file folder across the table. Vincent looked at him briefly before opening the folder and scanning its contents. "Adrian Bernal. I'm looking for him and I can't find him."

"And you think he works for me?" Vincent asked.

Recker shook his head. "No. I just figured you might have better luck in finding him than I have."

"And your interest in him?"

"Case I'm working on."

Vincent threw his hands up, thinking there must've been more to it. "There must be something else at stake. You're willing to kill a powerful player in the underworld in order to find this hoodlum?"

"He's planning on killing a cop. Officer Perez," Recker said.

"And you know this officer?"

"Nope. Never laid eyes on him."

"Then what's the connection?"

"There isn't one. Bernal's a bad dude, looking to kill an innocent person. Perez is a good cop, trying to do his job the best he can. I'm just trying to prevent a bad thing happening to a good person. There's nothing more to it than that."

Vincent smiled, believing him totally. "It's one of the things I've always admired about you. Your sense of morality. You're like a light in a sea of darkness, just trying to break through. You're an honorable man, Mike. You live by a certain code, your own code. I've always respected you."

"So, we have a deal?"

"Perhaps. Far be it for me to assume there's more in play here, so you'll have to excuse my skepticism. But you're willing to kill a man like Jeremiah, which is no easy task by the way, just for help in a case you're working, albeit one of good intentions?"

"There may be more to it than I've laid out and it may not be as simple as I've made it out to be," Recker said. "But I've got my own reasons for wanting Jeremiah dead and they're kind of personal, so I'm not really too keen on sharing right now."

"Understood."

"So, do we have a deal?" Recker asked.

With a smug look on his face, Vincent nodded, moving his mouth around as he swallowed the last part of his food. He called Malloy down to their table and handed him the file folder.

"Adrian Bernal," Vincent said. "Find him."

"Right away," Malloy said.

"Enjoy the rest of your meal," Vincent said, smiling. "We'll find him."

"He's not as easy as you might think," Recker said. "I've tried all the spots."

"Well, we'll go over them again. Just in case."

"What makes you think you'll succeed in the spots I didn't?"

"Well, we may be a bit more persuasive than you were."

11

It'd been about fifteen hours since Recker had his dinner meeting with Vincent. Recker and his cohorts had been working since around seven, putting most of their resources into getting a fix on Jeremiah's trail. Jones, though, wasn't sure it was the best use of their time. He wanted to split their efforts and still focus on Bernal, not wanting to solely leave it up to Vincent to find him. As they were working, Recker periodically looked over at his partner, and could see by the pained expressions on his face that he was bothered by something.

"So? What's eating you?" Recker asked.

"Do you really think it's wise to just abandon our search for Bernal?" Jones said.

"We're not abandoning it. We're just enlisting other resources in our efforts."

"For the last few hours, all we've done is try to get a

beat on Jeremiah. I'm not comfortable not seeing what's happening on the other fronts."

"David, what do you want to do? We tried our best. We tried everything we could. We came up empty. What else is there?"

"I don't know. I would just like to know and see what is being done instead of being left in the dark."

"When there's news to report I'm sure we'll hear something," Recker said.

"You're putting a lot of faith in Vincent to find him."

"Why shouldn't I? Has he ever not come through for us when we asked him for something?"

Jones sighed, agreeing with the sentiment, even though he still didn't like it much. "No, I suppose not."

"He did rescue us from that maniac," Mia said.

"Yes, I know," Jones said. "It doesn't mean I have to give him carte blanche over all our activities for the rest of our days though."

They continued working for a few more hours, still focusing on Jeremiah, much to Jones' chagrin. They tried to piece together news reports, public records, witness accounts and contacts in order to find where Jeremiah may have been hiding out. When Recker's phone rang, he and Jones eagerly looked at it, thinking Vincent had found their man. It wasn't what they were expecting though.

"Tyrell?" Recker said.

"Hey. Sorry I didn't get back to you sooner. Had a lot of things going on."

"It's not a problem. What's up?"

"I know you and Jeremiah got this thing going on right now and I'm getting caught up in the middle of it."

"Why, what's going on?"

"You're asking me to look for him. He's asking me to look for you. What the hell's going on with you guys?" Tyrell asked.

"He didn't tell you?"

"Nah, man, just said something about you double crossing him. I know that don't sound like you."

"He wanted me to kill Vincent," Recker said.

"Oh, wow. He didn't say nothing about that."

"I didn't figure he would."

"Did you say you would do it?"

"Yeah. Only because he was trying to blackmail me. Had to figure out a plan first."

"Blackmail you? How?"

"He was threatening to kill someone I know unless I did it. He had men following them."

"The prof?"

"No. Someone else."

Tyrell sighed, trying to figure out what he was going to do. "Listen, he wants me to try and draw you out somewhere."

"Why?"

"Why you think? To put a bullet in you, probably."

"Well that's not very nice," Recker said, joking.

"Yeah, it's all fun and games for you. I'm the one getting caught up in the middle here."

"Listen, Tyrell, I know you do business with both of us

and you don't wanna sell either of us out. I'm not asking you to compromise yourself."

"Then what do you want me to do?"

"Give me something I can use. If he double crossed me, what makes you think he won't do the same to you sometime? You're not part of his crew either."

"I live out here, man. I deal with these guys every day, you don't," Tyrell said.

"I know. But I'll make it worth it for you if you give me something though. And I give you my word nothing will ever come back to you."

"You know sometimes I wish I never met you."

Recker laughed, thinking it wasn't the first time he'd heard that. "Congratulations. You just joined my fan club."

"What do you want?"

"Where can I find him? Where does he go? The only place I know is the house in Upper Darby where he meets me."

"Yeah, he won't show up there again for a while, probably. He's got places like that all over the city. Probably a dozen or so. He doesn't like to conduct business in the same place all the time in case someone plans to surprise him, know what I mean? Yeah. I can give you a few addresses but it probably won't do you any good."

"Gotta start somewhere."

"All right, I'll text you the places and you can do whatever you wanna do."

"Sounds good," Recker said.

"But listen, you better get him, you understand? Cause if you don't, and he kills you, and he finds out I was helping you, I'm probably gonna be joining you in whatever plot you wind up in."

"What? You wouldn't enjoy spending the rest of eternity together?"

"Hell no."

"Any other spots besides these meeting houses?"

"Uh, yeah, there's some nightclubs he likes to frequent sometimes," Tyrell said. "Good luck if you wanna take him out in one of those though."

"Why? What's so special about it?"

"Well when he goes to those places he's got ten, sometimes twenty guys with him. Man, you'll never get near him. Especially if you're public enemy number one. As soon as you show up, you'll get bullets flying from every direction at you."

"You let me worry about that."

"I didn't say I was worried. I'm just telling you. Plus, those places are packed. You kill him in there and you'll be wanted all over town."

"Wanted by who? The police? They already want me. Nothing would change."

"I guess. If you take out Jeremiah, it's gonna leave a clear path for Vincent you know," Tyrell mentioned.

"I know."

"He's gonna have all the power."

"I know."

"I'm just saying."

"Would that bother you?" Recker asked. "You work for him sometimes."

"I dunno, I guess it'd be OK. I'd just have to pick up more work from him to compensate for Jeremiah."

"Don't worry about it. Like I said, I'll make sure you're taken care of."

As soon as Recker hung up, he put the phone down on the table as he waited for some of the addresses Tyrell had told him about. While waiting, he explained to Jones and Mia what his conversation with Tyrell was about.

"Were you on the debate team in high school?" Mia said. "Because you have a gift for getting people to change their mind on things."

"No, I was on the archery squad."

"No surprise there."

"And I don't think I really did much to change his mind," Recker said. "I think he knows if Jeremiah did it to me, he'd do it to him."

After a few more moments, Recker's phone started going off. It was texts from Tyrell listing some of the addresses Jeremiah used for meetings. He also listed a few of the nightclubs he knew Jeremiah liked to go to. Recker grabbed a piece of paper and started writing them down so they could put them through the computer and start analyzing the locations. As they started plugging the addresses in, Jones had one final thought about locating Bernal, not wanting to give up on it.

"Can we try one last thing with Bernal?" Jones asked.

"Are you still on that?" Recker said.

"Humor me for a second."

"If you want."

"Try having another talk with his girlfriend, Maria Guerrero."

"As me or as Detective Scarborough?"

"As your detective alter ego," Jones said.

"Why? What good would it do? She already blew me off once."

"She may be more willing to talk this time around."

"What makes you think that?" Recker asked, not seeing how the second time would be better than the first.

"If Maria Guerrero knows a man like Vincent is coming after her boyfriend, knowing his reputation, she may be more willing to help you out in finding him before Vincent does."

"David, I think it's a waste of time. Just let Vincent do what we agreed to let him do. Why are you so adamant about not giving Vincent the opportunity to do what we couldn't?"

"Because Officer Perez's life is at stake. And I'm still worried about whether Vincent will be able to find him either. Or whether he'll have the same sense of urgency we do. After all, how willing or eager is Vincent at saving the life of a police officer?" Jones said. "They're not exactly on the same side you know."

"Well, technically, neither are we."

"There is a fundamental difference between Vincent and us. I'm sure I don't need to explain it to you any further."

"Fine. If it'll make you happy, I'll go to Guerrero's house again, OK?" Recker said finally, seeing how important it seemed to be to Jones.

"That's all I ask."

"And if she gives me nothing again?"

"If she doesn't tell you anything, then I'll stop harping on it and leave it alone from now on."

"You will?" Recker asked, not sure he believed it.

"I give you my word. If you get nothing of value, then I promise I won't say another word about it and let Vincent work his course, for better or for worse."

"All right. I'll give it one more shot with her. Then I'm checking a few of these houses that are on Jeremiah's list."

"Noted," Jones said.

Recker made sure he was loaded up, taking a few extra guns more than usual, just in case he ran into trouble at any of the addresses Tyrell had provided. He bid adieu to Jones and Mia and left the office, hopeful he'd come back with more information than he'd left with. After Recker was gone, Jones looked at Mia, thinking she was handling everything very well. She didn't seem to be fazed by any of the work they were doing, or how they talked, or what they planned on doing. She was much calmer about everything than Jones had expected.

"I must say you're doing a good job in handling your emotions," Jones said.

"Huh? What emotions?"

"Well, if you and Mike proceed with your relationship, then I have to say I admire how calm you seem. He goes out and meets crime bosses, and criminals, and dangerous people, men with guns who could try to kill him, but you don't outwardly show any worries."

"And you're surprised?" she asked.

"Truthfully, yes."

"Well I don't see how it'd do any good for me to be hanging all over him and telling him to be careful and all that. He already knows to be."

"I agree."

"I don't know. I guess I don't want to be one of those girlfr—well, whatever it is I am," Mia said, stopping short of labeling herself since she still wasn't positive yet what their relationship was. "I guess I figure if I keep harping on him to be careful, and worrying about him, and crying on his shoulder, then it gets his focus off what it should be on and onto me."

"I must say I admire your attitude," Jones said.

"I know how good he is, it's not like he's someone who's not experienced or something. If he's out there worrying about me and what I think, then I know that's probably when he'd end up getting hurt. I can't say I'm not worried or I never will be, but I can't let it show."

"Well, there's nothing wrong with showing worry and concern. As long as you don't let it become a sticking point. That's when it would become a problem," Jones said, offering some advice.

Recker's first stop after leaving the office was Maria Guerrero's home. Just as he did the first time he was there, he parked down the street and kept an eye out on the place. In the event Bernal doubled back to the comfort of his girlfriend's house, Recker didn't want to make the potential mistake of barging in and scaring his target away without knowing whether he was actually there or not. Recker sat there for two hours, just watching, and waiting and, without seeing a stitch of movement, decided he'd had enough of that. He got out of his car and walked to the Guerrero house and pounded on the door. Much to Recker's surprise, the door was answered much quicker this time. He only had to knock a couple of times before Guerrero came to the door.

"Hi, rememb...," Recker said, stopping when he saw the side of Guerrero's face.

Her face was swollen and bruised, and her eye was puffy. Gone was the overconfident and cocky person that he talked to before, and instead was replaced by a battered and beaten woman. She looked despondent in her current condition.

"Do you remember me?" Recker asked, concerned for her wellbeing.

"Yes," she said with a single nod of her head.

"Are you OK? Do you need help?"

Guerrero shook her head and shrugged, seeming indifferent. "What do you want?" she asked, holding her face, without a shred of the spirit she showed in their first encounter.

"Who did that to you?"

She shook her head again, not wanting to go into it. "Nobody."

"I know you didn't just run into a wall or something," Recker said.

"It doesn't matter. There's nothing you can do."

"Did Adrian do it?"

She shook her head once again, a painful expression overtaking her face. "No, it wasn't him."

"Then who?"

"Please, it doesn't matter."

Recker took her at her word it wasn't Bernal who had beaten her face to a pulp. But if it wasn't him, he wondered who else would have done it to her. It could've been one of his conspirators, but Recker figured it was a long shot, assuming whoever did it would've had to answer to Bernal for their misdeeds. Considering how she acted to him before, and she was most likely hiding the fugitive, even if she only knew where he was, he probably shouldn't have been as interested in her misfortunes as he was. But Recker ignored it all. What he saw right now was a beaten, humbled woman standing in front of him. After thinking about it, Recker thought he might have had the answer. He pulled out his phone and tapped into a computer database they used in the office Jones allowed him to be hooked up to. He scrolled through some pictures of the more well known, less than scrupulous, criminals the city had to offer. He stopped at the one he thought might have done this to Guerrero. Recker turned his phone around and showed her the picture.

"This didn't happen to be the guy, was it?" Recker asked.

Guerrero took a look at the picture but quickly looked away, not wanting to spend another second having to see the man's face again. The agonizing look on her face told Recker all he needed, without her having to say a word or confirm it really was him.

"Please go away," she said somberly.

"I can help you if you tell me where Adrian is now," Recker said.

"I... I don't know."

Recker couldn't tell anymore whether she was being truthful or not. Before it was easy to tell she was lying. Now, she just seemed like she wanted to curl up in a corner somewhere. "If you don't, some innocent people are going to wind up getting hurt."

"What's it look like to you right now?"

"I can help if you let me."

"If I knew anything, don't you think I would've already told the guy who did this?"

Recker wasn't sure how else, if at all, he could get through to her. He didn't have much more of a chance though. Before he could think of anything else, Guerrero ended the conversation by giving him a smile, then calmly closed the door on him. Recker walked back to his car, and though he wasn't happy the woman had been beaten, was content with his efforts. There wasn't much more he could do, especially if she wasn't willing to cooperate. Before Recker got going with his other business, he called Jones to let him know what happened and to inform him he was moving on.

"Looks like we close the books on Bernal," Recker said.

"The girlfriend still won't talk, huh?" Jones asked.

"No. She was much more pleasant about it this time, though."

"Oh?"

"I guess it's tough to be snarky when half your face is black and blue."

"Black and blue?"

"You didn't…"

"Of course *I* didn't," Recker said, anticipating where Jones was going with that.

"I should hope not."

"I didn't. But somebody sure did."

"One of Adrian Bernal's associates no doubt," Jones said.

"No, I don't think so."

"Why not?"

"I showed her a few pictures. A couple she had no reaction to. But one, one she could hardly look at. She turned away instead of looking at it."

"Whose picture was it?"

"Jimmy Malloy."

"I guess it means Vincent's making good on his promise," Jones said.

"He did say he could be more persuasive than us."

"I would've hoped it meant not beating up on women, though. I guess nothing's off limits to them."

"Not much," Recker said. "At least we know they're working the case though."

"What about Maria Guerrero?"

"What about her? I asked if she knew where Bernal was. I asked if I could help her. She still won't talk or accept help. There's nothing else we can do for her. You can only help people who'll let you."

"I know. I guess that's that then."

"Seems so."

"Are you satisfied now?" Recker asked. "Can you accept Vincent's on it? Can we move on?"

Jones sighed, still not liking it, but agreed anyway. "Yes. What are your plans now?"

"Stake out a couple houses on Tyrell's list."

"When you say stake out, you mean?"

"Well, we'll just see how it plays out."

12

———

Recker's first stop was an address on sixty-second Street. As he usually did, he parked down the street to survey the area for a while. The address actually wasn't a house and appeared to be a vacant building. It had two roll up bay doors, along with an entrance door, giving Recker the impression it was possibly an auto repair garage at one time, or maybe some type of shipping business. In any case, there was some graffiti on the bay doors and he didn't notice any kind of activity going on to indicate it was a thriving or active business.

Jones had gotten back to him with information on the building after digging into records and confirmed it did indeed used to be an auto garage. But it'd been closed for several years. The current owner of the building wasn't listed as Jeremiah, and the name on the lease didn't appear to have any connections to him, at least no obvious ones. It was possible one of Jeremiah's men had taken care of the contractual obligations to leave his name off it. Recker just sat and waited, hoping something would catch his eye at some point. If not, he'd eventually just break in somehow and see if there was anything inside which would give him some information into Jeremiah's business dealings. Luckily for him, he wouldn't have to resort to such dealings.

After a couple hours of waiting, he observed an expensive looking black SUV pull up, parking along the curb near the front of the building. Four men piled out of the car and milled around on the sidewalk by the door for a few minutes, seemingly joking around with each other. One of the men eventually pulled out a set of keys and unlocked the door, allowing the others with him to enter the facility. Recker gave them an hour to themselves before he decided to approach the building, just in case they had more visitors coming. He also wanted to make sure there was nobody else already inside the building, though he made what he thought was a safe assumption that there wasn't, considering they had to unlock the doors themselves. As he approached the building, Recker continuously looked around, just in case there were lookouts on the perimeter. Since there didn't appear to be any, he walked right up to the glass door and started pounding on it. Within a few seconds one of the men he recognized from the car came up to the door. He opened it just a little so he could see who the stranger was.

"What do you want, man?"

"Oh, I just came here to deliver a pizza," Recker said.

"What?"

"Pizza. Someone here order a pizza?"

The man looked at Recker like he was crazy. "No, no one here ordered a pizza!"

"Oh, my mistake. I must have the wrong address."

"You don't even have a pizza."

"Oh, I left it in the car till I made sure I had the right place."

"Well you got the wrong place. Hit the road, bud."

"Sure, no problem. Could you just look at this and let me know where this is before I go," Recker said, reaching into his coat for something.

The man didn't want to help him with anything and looked perturbed about Recker wasting his time and was about to shut the door in his face. Recker removed his gun from inside his coat and fired point blank at the man's chest, putting a couple holes in it. As the man fell backwards from the blast, Recker stepped over the man's dead body as he quickly identified where the other men were. There was a small folding card table in the middle of the room where the other three men were sitting. There were a few handguns on the table along with some sandwiches. As soon as the men heard the gunfire at the door and saw their friend fall, they jumped to their feet, grabbing their weapons. Recker fired a couple rounds, hitting two of them immediately, though not fatally. With bullets heading back in his direction, Recker took cover behind a small counter near the front door. It must have been a cashier station left over from its previous life.

The good news for Recker was, even though he was outnumbered, the other men didn't have much to take cover behind. There was actually nothing other than the small card table, which they flipped up on its side and crouched behind, though it didn't really offer much protection. It was tough for them to get any kind of shot off without exposing at least half their body. One of the men Recker shot in the thigh and the other got hit in the left arm. There was a brief lull in the action lasting about five seconds as the participants reloaded their weapons. Recker peeked over the counter and saw he had an opportunity to pick off the first person who showed their head. He pointed his gun, waiting for his next victim. The man to the far left of him was the first to raise up in anticipation of firing, though he never got the chance to. As soon as his body rose above the table, Recker blew a hole through the middle of his chest. Seeing their friend shot dead next to them angered the remaining two and spurred them into trying to avenge his death. They both fired furiously at the counter Recker was hiding behind, causing him to get down and take cover. He crawled to his left and the end of the counter, waiting for the right opportunity to strike. The last two of his targets continued firing at the counter, hoping the bullets would pierce through the wood and somehow find a way through and into Recker's body. They had no such luck, however.

Recker emerged from the side of the counter, firing away at the two men, catching them by surprise. The first man got hit in the shoulder and went down, then the man on the right got shot in the stomach and hunched over as blood started pouring out of his midsection. Recker got to his feet and quickly made his way over to the bodies of the remaining survivors. As the man in the middle, who was clutching his wounded shoulder saw his shooter standing over him, he reached for his gun. His weapon had dropped from his hand when he was shot and wound up laying only a few inches away from him. Recker noticed and kicked the gun away, the weapon sliding across the concrete floor until it hit the far wall. Recker pointed his gun at the man's head as he gave him a couple options.

"You got two choices," Recker said. "You can live or you can die. It's real simple."

"Screw you," the man whispered through gritted teeth against the pain, sweat beading on his face.

"Tell me where I can find Jeremiah and you'll be the only one that walks out of here. Or you can clam up like a good soldier and get buried with your buddies."

"Once Jeremiah finds out I sold him out I'll wind up next to them, anyway. That's no deal."

"Not if I kill him before he finds out."

"I ain't telling you nothing."

Recker straightened his arm out as he steadied the weapon, aiming at the man's chest. "Last chance."

The wounded man just looked away, not interested in the deal that Recker offered. A man of his word, Recker pulled the trigger and helped the man meet his dead friends. He heard the last survivor groaning, keeled over on his knees, and clutching his stomach, blood staining his hands and arms, not to mention the gray concrete underneath him. Though Recker assumed it would be a waste of time, he offered the guy the same deal as the last one.

"What about you?" Recker asked. "You feel like talking or you feel like dying?"

"I'm dead, anyway. I know I ain't gonna be able to make it to no hospital."

"I can call an ambulance real quick."

"Nah, I'm a loyal soldier. I'd rather die than betray my friends."

"Suit yourself."

Recker knew it was a lost cause trying to convince him otherwise and pointed his gun at the back of the man's head. He pulled the trigger, and the man slumped forward onto the ground. Recker took one last look at all the bodies just to make sure none of them were still breathing, and they couldn't give him a last second surprise. After confirming they were all dead, he took a look around the place to see if the thugs had any papers lying around which would give a clue as to where Jeremiah was now. The place was pretty scarce though, and there wasn't much to even check. There was a back office to the rear of the building with a desk and a filing cabinet Recker searched through, but the only things he found were meaningless papers. Nothing which would indicate where Jeremiah was or give away any of his business dealings. He took one last look around the building to make sure he didn't miss anything, then he also checked the dead bodies to see if they had any papers on them. Still nothing. He took a phone out of one of the dead men's pockets and scrolled through it, hoping he could get something from it. He saw a contact listing for Jeremiah and thought about calling it to let him know he was coming, but thought better of it. He figured once he took out some of his men, Jeremiah would get the word Recker was coming. There was no need to alert him beforehand and get his men hyped that Recker would be coming. With his work there finished, Recker started on his way to the next address on the list. As he walked out the door, he picked up his phone and called 911.

"What is your emergency?" the operator asked.

"Yeah, I'd like to report a shooting. There's four dead bodies inside a vacant building."

"What's the address?"

Recker gave the address then hung up. By contacting the police, he assumed Jeremiah would get the word that he hit his place rather quickly. He called Jones to let him know of the trouble he'd ran into at the first stop, and to let him know he was still alive and kicking.

"I'm heading to the second location now," Recker said.

"Anything of note at the first spot?" Jones asked.

"Uh, yeah, four dead bodies."

"Were they dead when you found them?"

"Nope."

Jones sighed, hoping he wasn't going to leave a trail of bodies everywhere he went. "Do you really think it's wise to be so public with this? Jeremiah will surely know it was you."

"That's what I'm counting on," Recker said.

"Why? Why do you want him to be ready for you?"

"Because I want him to know I'm coming. I want him to know I'm dismantling him and his crew one stop at a time. He threatened me, he threatened someone I care about. I'm not just gonna roll over and tickle him. I want him to know hell's coming."

"It surely is."

"Mike, just be careful," Mia said, listening on the speakerphone.

"Don't worry. It's not my time to go yet."

"Did you check if there was anything left behind we could use to get a fix on Jeremiah's location?" Jones asked.

"Yeah, there wasn't much there. It didn't look like a place they spent much time at. Probably just a spot to conduct business then leave immediately afterwards."

"I wouldn't be surprised if it's what all these addresses are," Jones said.

"Could be. It might be all Tyrell knows, the meeting places. He might not have been to any of Jeremiah's strongholds."

"Well, I've already pulled up your next stop," Jones said, looking at a picture of the house on the computer. "It's an end unit row home in West Philly."

"Is it boarded up?" Recker asked.

"It is."

Recker told his partner he'd let him know when his business was concluded after the next stop. He had a feeling it would be an almost identical situation as the first one. And Recker was just fine with that. In fact, as far as he was concerned, the more bodies piling up, the better he liked it. As long as his wasn't one of them. The more he thought about everything, the angrier he got about it. Now, he didn't want to just kill Jeremiah, he wanted to cripple his organization first, then kill him. He wanted

Jeremiah to worry about him coming before he got there. Recker figured it would make killing Jeremiah much more satisfying. This was the side of Recker, Jones worried about. When this part of his personality emerged, the one that enjoyed being The Silencer, Jones knew there wasn't much he could do to stop it. All he could really do was get out of the way and hope nothing bad happened to Recker, because he knew plenty of bad things were going to happen to the people who happened to stand in his way.

When Recker got to the row home in West Philly, just like usual, he waited an hour or so to survey the area. Almost immediately, he saw a few men hanging around out front on the porch, alternating between there and inside the house. He saw three different guys go in and out of the house within the hour. Recker was assuming there was more. One thing he knew about Jeremiah was, he never seemed to travel light. In every situation Recker could think of where he interacted with Jeremiah, or members of his gang, there were always at least four of them. Whenever he met with Jeremiah, at the former auto garage, the men trailing Mia, there were always at least four. He figured this place would be no different.

Recker took a few minutes to think of his plan before he walked over to it. He assumed he'd have to improvise once the bullets started flying, but he wanted to at least have something to start with. Once he got out of his car and started walking toward the home, he noticed someone looking out through the upstairs window, which was not boarded-up. It was actually the only window of the house with open glass. Recker figured it must have been the lookout station, the guy who warned everyone inside if trouble was coming. If that was the case, then they'd all know he was coming well before he got to the front door. As he walked on the concrete sidewalk leading up by the house, nobody was on the porch. But as he started up the steps leading to the front door of the house, two men came out to see what he wanted.

"Far enough," one man said, with a gun firmly visible and planted in the front of his pants, inside the waistband. "What do you want?"

"I have a message from Jeremiah," Recker said. "He told me to bring it over right away."

The man looked at Recker eyebrows squeezing together, not knowing a thing about it. "He didn't say anything about you coming."

"Well, he was worried about phones being tapped. So he had me do it old school."

"OK. So, what's the message?"

"Well, he told me to only give it to the guy in charge."

"What's it about?"

"Something about the woman he was having tailed. You guys know about that?"

"Yeah, we know."

"The guys tailing her were killed, and she escaped. We think we got a location on her and I think he was giving you guys the assignment."

The man sighed and rolled his eyes, thinking he was being a pain. "Get Stash out here," he said to the other man out there with him.

Just a few seconds later, the man emerged with the

third man of the group, a bald-headed man, tough look-ing, goatee, looked like a weightlifter. He also had a visible gun in the waistband of his pants. Seemed to be a staple of this crew. The leader looked the stranger up and down, giving Recker the impression maybe the man recognized him as The Silencer. If he did, Recker was going to have to come up shooting in a hurry.

"You got a message from Jeremiah?" the leader asked.

"Sure do."

"I don't recognize you."

"Oh, well, I'm kinda new. He just started using me last week," Recker said.

The man seemed satisfied enough, though he still didn't look best pleased. "All right, what do you got? Let's see it."

"OK, I'm, uh, gonna reach my hand in," Recker said, pointing to his coat, acting nervous so they wouldn't consider him a threat and he could get the jump on them. "I'm gonna reach in and get the message."

"Just do it."

Recker laughed, "OK. Just wanted to make sure you guys weren't trigger happy," he said, pretending to struggle in finding the note. "So how many guys you got in there, anyway?"

"None of your business. Jeremiah must be scraping the bottom of the barrel if he's hiring guys like you these days," the leader said sarcastically, growing impatient.

"Oh, here it is," Recker said, putting his fingers on the handle of his gun. "I got it."

Recker quickly pulled out his weapon, catching the

three men off guard. His first shot hit the leader in the chest, then in a matter of seconds, turned toward the other two and hit the both of them before they were able to withdraw their guns. Without knowing how many were inside, Recker hurried to the door before he had company. Before going inside, he couldn't take the chance of any of the three men on the porch sneaking up on him inside. He had to make sure they'd all stay down permanently. Without a second thought, he delivered a headshot to each of the three gang members, though as it turned out, two of them were already dead so it didn't matter but, 'better be safe than sorry' as his old daddy used to say. It gave him peace of mind knowing he wouldn't have to worry about them again.

Recker returned to the screen door, throwing it open as he stood in the doorway, ready to fire. As soon as he showed himself, a bullet whizzed by him, ripping through the mesh screen in the door. Recker quickly identified where the shot came from, locating a man standing on the second floor, at the top of the steps. He returned fire, grazing the man in the leg, dropping him to his knees. The man cried out in pain and grabbed for his legs, though he knew he had to dispatch of the dangerous man at the door before he came up and finished the job. As he brought his gun up and tried to aim at the man in the door, Recker took aim himself. He fired a couple more rounds, both of which found its intended target. The man at the top of the stairs lost his balance as the bullets ripped through his insides and proceeded to tumble violently down the steps. The man came to his final resting spot just in front of Recker. He was flat on his back with his arms outstretched, blood soaking through his white shirt. Recker gave him a nudge with his foot to make sure he was gone. He was.

All was quiet for a few moments. Recker wasn't quite sure which he preferred, the deathly silence or the action-fueled haze of gunfire and bullets flying all around him. At least when people were shooting at him he knew what to expect. He worried more when he wasn't sure what was around the corner or lurking in the shadows. As he stepped into the living room, he immediately noticed this house seemed to have more furnishings than the others he'd been in so far. There was actually a couch, some tables, and a few lamps. It actually looked like people spent time there instead of using it for a few minutes for a transaction then leaving for somewhere else. Recker cautiously and methodically went through every room on the first floor, ready for more shooting practice. Luckily for them, nobody else was present.

Recker then proceeded to go up the steps to the second floor. Once he reached the top step, he heard a noise coming from the first bedroom to his right. The door was closed, leading Recker to believe somebody was in there. The rest of the rooms on the floor, two other bedrooms, and a bathroom, had their doors open. Recker quickly swept his way through them to clear them before returning to the room with the closed door. He assumed he was going to be met with gunfire the moment he opened the door, maybe even once he jiggled the handle. Recker figured he'd bypass all that and quietly stepped toward the door then forcefully kicked it open. A gun fired, and a bullet lodged into the swinging door. Recker took a step inside the room and found his next target, ready to pounce on him. Just as he was about to squeeze the trigger, though, he let up and took his finger off it. The person who fired the shot at him looked awfully young. He looked like he was just a kid, couldn't have been more than sixteen years old. Seeing someone like Recker pointing a gun right at his head, the kid looked beyond terrified and dropped his own gun as he waited for the inevitable from the dangerous man.

"How old are you, son?" Recker asked.

"Sixteen."

"Your folks know you're here?"

The kid, still looking scared as could be, shook his head.

"What are you doing here with these people? How long you been here?"

"They were just initiating me this week."

"Is this really the kind of life you want?"

The kid just looked at the floor and shrugged. "What's your mom think about all this?"

"She's worried about me 'cause I dropped out of school."

"You know anything about the man you're working for, Jeremiah?" Recker asked.

"Not really. Just what they tell me."

"Well, I'll tell you now, there ain't no future in it. I'm putting him out of business."

The kid nodded, not sure what the man was going to do with him.

"You know who I am?" Recker asked.

"No, sir," the kid said.

"They call me The Silencer. You heard of me?"

Not knowing what to say, the kid nodded again.

"You wanna die before you hit seventeen?" Recker asked.

"No."

"Because if I was of that mind, you'd be joining your friends out there."

The kid nodded again, knowing the man could've killed him easily by now. "Are you gonna let me go?"

"It kind of depends on you," Recker said. "If you were two or three years older, you'd be dead already because I'd have killed you the minute I laid eyes on you."

"Yes, sir."

"I'm gonna give you a second chance, which I don't give many people."

"Thank you."

"I don't want thanks. I just don't wanna see you out on these streets again with a gun in your hands," Recker said. "You go home, hug your mom, get back in school, and do what she tells you. You do that, you'll be alright."

"I will," the kid said, running past him to get out of the house as quickly as possible.

Recker stopped him before he got out of sight though. "Hey," he said, stopping the kid in his tracks. "I mean what I said. I catch you next week or next year running with some thugs again, and you got a gun, next time I'm pulling the trigger. And you'll make your mom a very unhappy woman. You understand me?"

The kid nodded, "Yeah."

"Go on, get out of here."

Recker wasn't sure if his little talk would really do any good, or whether it would just fall on deaf ears, but at least he tried to help a young kid out. He showed a little compassion, which should've made Jones happy. He looked through the one open window and saw the kid fly out of the house and down the street. He wanted to make sure he didn't misjudge the kid and just send him downstairs and allow him to wait for Recker as he descended the stairs, giving him some free shots at him. Knowing there was nobody left in the house alive, Recker started looking around the house, going through each room for clues as to Jeremiah's whereabouts. He knew he didn't have a lot of time though, as he figured somebody would've reported the shots by now, and possibly the dead bodies if someone saw the activities on the front porch. He assumed the police would be there within a few minutes so he only quickly looked through each room in the obvious spots to see if something was lying around in plain sight. Once he was satisfied there wasn't anything to find, and as he thought he was running out of time, he started to leave. He walked out the front door and stood on the porch, looking up and down the street for signs of the police. Surprisingly, there was nothing coming yet. He stood between two of the dead bodies and looked down at them.

"I'm surprised you guys fell for that," Recker said, referring to the note trick they fell for.

As he walked down the steps, he heard sirens in the background. He assumed the police were on their way. Recker turned the corner at the front of the property and started walking down the sidewalk. Within another minute, a few police cruisers came driving by him. Recker turned his head away from the street and coughed to hide his face from the officers driving by. Once he got to his car, he sat there for a while and watched the police activity at the house. He also called Jones to let him know to scratch another one off the list.

"I take it there were no problems?" Jones asked.

"I guess it depends on what you define as a problem. It was nothing I couldn't handle."

"I almost hesitate to ask, but I guess I should, how many bodies should I be aware of?"

"Uh, let's see... uh, four."

"You can't remember? Do you need some extra time to think about it?"

"No, it was four," Recker said. "Well, it was actually five. But I only killed four."

"Oh, you let one get away. You must be losing your touch," Jones said sarcastically.

"No, I'm not losing my touch. One was a kid, probably fifteen or sixteen. I gave him a little speech, then sent him packing."

"Well, it was very sporting of you."

"I don't know about that. I just hope it did the kid

some good and I never have to see him again. I let him off with a warning. Hopefully, it'll be enough."

"Well, you gave him a second chance. That's more than some people get. The rest will be on him. I hope he takes it."

"Yeah." Recker sighed. "I guess it's on to the next address."

"Why don't you come back to the office and recharge for a bit?" Jones asked, not wanting Recker to overexert himself.

"I'm OK."

"Mike, you can't wage a war and win it in one day. You've taken out eight of his men, stormed two of his meeting spots, you've sent him a message. If you keep going from house to house, eventually they'll be waiting for you. And they'll be shooting first."

Though Recker didn't want to admit it, he thought Jones might have had a point. "Yeah, maybe you're right."

"We've already crossed two off the list. Let's see how it shakes out before we make our next move," Jones said. "Maybe he'll do something crazy or desperate in response and make him play right into our hands."

"It might be wishful thinking, but OK, we'll give it a try."

13

─────────

By the time Recker had gotten back to the office, it was well after dinner. Though he agreed with Jones' premise of waiting to see if Jeremiah would make a move, he still was a little amped up and was ready for another battle immediately. He drove around for a while, hoping something else would come up he could deal with right away. Part of why he was so anxious to keep moving was that he knew what an inconvenience it was to Mia, having a death threat hanging over her head, and hiding out in a strange office indefinitely. He wanted to try to simplify her life as quickly as possible, even though he knew it wasn't likely to end this war right away. But Jones was right, he couldn't keep barging through every front door he came across. Eventually they'd be waiting for him and wouldn't fall for anything in his bag of tricks, they'd simply shoot first before he had a chance to open his mouth.

As soon as Recker entered the office, Mia ran over to

him and hugged him. She wanted to give him a kiss, but figured she'd save it for another time, when there wasn't as much going on. She didn't want to overwhelm him with personal stuff when she knew he had other things on his mind.

"I'm glad you're back," Mia said.

"And in one piece," Jones said.

"Just another day at the office." Recker shrugged it off.

"Did you eat yet?" Mia asked.

"No. Haven't had time."

"We haven't either. I'll fix us some sandwiches."

Mia went to the refrigerator and got out the lunch meat to make the three of them dinner. Recker was starting to feel some exhaustion from the day's events. He sat down on the couch and looked up at the ceiling and tried to wind down a little. It was tough for him to block everything out of his mind, though, and replayed his last two stops in his head a few times. He looked over at Mia and was thinking about how well she seemed to be handling everything. She didn't give any outward signs of worry about herself. He admired her for how strong she seemed to be. Not a lot of people would act as calm as she was.

After they ate dinner, they sat around and started making plans for the following day. They still had a bunch of addresses for Recker to check out, though Jones wasn't sure it was such a good idea anymore. After what happened today, there was no way Jeremiah's men wouldn't be waiting for Recker to strike at any of the locations. Jones didn't feel it was even remotely possible Recker would have the same success as he did.

"After what happened today, do you really believe you're going to find anything at any of these locations?" Jones asked, holding the paper up that had the addresses on it.

"Maybe not. That doesn't mean it won't be worthwhile though."

"I guess it would depend on what we're talking about. Are we talking about trying to find Jeremiah and ending this as quickly as possible? Or are we talking about finding as many of his men as possible and killing all of them along the way? Which is it?"

"A little bit of both maybe," Recker said.

"Mike, this isn't a both situation. Finding and eliminating Jeremiah should be the only consideration. With him, it ends. It's not about killing his soldiers," Jones said. "Once he's gone, they will no longer be a threat. They won't go against you without his orders."

"That's kind of a big assumption, don't you think?"

"No, I don't. I think it's a reasonable assumption. You don't need to wage war against everybody. Just one man."

"That's what I'm doing."

"And what do you think will happen if you go to one of these houses and they are waiting for you? Instead of four or five guys, they lure you in, and inside they have twenty guys. What then?"

"Then I'll deal with it."

"You're not invincible. What do you think will happen if you get yourself killed?"

"I guess I'll be dead."

"And Mia? What do you think will happen to her if you're gone?"

Recker looked at her, getting a warm smile from her in return. "You sure like to hit below the belt."

"Sometimes it's what's necessary to bring people to their knees and make them realize what's at stake and what's important," Jones said.

"Can I put my two cents in?" Mia asked, putting her hand up.

"Of course," Recker said, although he had a pretty good idea which side of the fence she'd fall on.

"I agree with David. There's no way they won't have some type of trap set for you at these other places."

"And do you have another suggestion?"

"Didn't Tyrell mention something about Jeremiah going to nightclubs?" she asked.

"Yeah."

"Wouldn't it be a better plan to try and take him out there instead?"

"Do you realize how tall a task that will be?" Recker asked.

"How many nightclubs can there be?"

"In Philadelphia? Hundreds."

"Really?" Mia asked, obviously not a member of the nightclub scene. "I thought there were maybe twenty or so."

"No. There's no way of knowing right now what clubs he likes to go to or what night he goes," Recker said.

"But Mia may be on to something," Jones said. "Just

hitting these houses on this list isn't going to accomplish anything, other than satisfying your thirst for blood. You're not going to find anything leading to Jeremiah in any of these places and the odds of you getting any of his men to talk or give him up are beyond... well, let's just say you'll have a better chance with a snowball you know where."

"OK. Even if I agree to forego the rest of this list, how are we gonna find out which nightclub he goes to?"

"Most nightclubs have security cameras, do they not?" Jones asked.

"Yeah."

Jones tilted his face and looked at him with his eyebrow raised. He waited for Recker to catch up.

"And you can hack into them," Recker said, finally getting up to speed.

"Once I get into their systems, I can start running facial recognition software over the past few weeks until we see which clubs he goes to. Maybe we can find a pattern. Maybe he rotates between a few clubs in particular."

"Plus, it'll keep him off balance," Mia said. "He'll be so worried and focused on you hitting these other houses that you'll throw him off when you don't show up."

Recker smiled at her, thinking she was a quick student. "You're learning quickly."

"I have the best teachers."

After they finished eating, Jones immediately got to work, trying to hack into every nightclub security system that he came across. He was sure he would be able to find

Jeremiah somewhere. It just might take some time to comb through all that footage. Once he was able to pull up footage from the first club, Recker and Mia started looking through the videos.

"How easy is it going to be to spot him?" Mia asked, not quite sure how the system worked.

"Well, there's several different ways to program the software," Jones said, explaining the intricacies of his system. "We can program it to run itself completely in search of an exact match based on the information I give it. In that case, we simply sit back and wait for it to beep when it's finished."

"That's easy enough."

"But, considering the complexity and urgency of this situation, I've loosened the parameters somewhat."

"How so?"

"It's possible he knows how to avoid cameras, or block them out, or have them disabled. So in this case, I've programmed it to look for even partial matches, that way we can sort out one way or another whether it's him. So you may get several false positives," Jones said.

"It's also possible he has so many people around him that a camera doesn't get a good shot of his face," Recker said. "Maybe it only gets a partial look at his face."

"Yes. In any case, the software will beep and pull up the pictures of the subject in question. Then it's up to us to quantify whether it's really him or just a lookalike."

"Gotcha," Mia said. "How long will all this take?"

"With the amount of clubs in this city? Probably days, maybe a week. It really depends on how much footage we go through," Jones said. "It will go faster with all three of us looking. If it was just me, as it usually is, it would most likely take longer."

"How far back did you set it?" Recker asked.

"A month. I assume that will be more than enough time. If he hasn't been there in a month, then it's most likely not a regular stop for him."

They spent the rest of the night combing through security footage from a couple different nightclubs. There were a couple of partial matches that the system flagged, though after closer inspection, it was determined that it wasn't Jeremiah. After four hours of looking at a computer screen, Jones needed a break and got up to turn the TV on.

"Problem?" Recker asked.

"Just stretching my legs a little," Jones said.

"Two clubs down, two hundred more to go."

"I suppose we'll get there in time."

As Jones sat down on the couch, his eyes glued to the television screen, Recker could see that there was something playing he was interested in. Wondering what was fascinating him so much, Recker also stopped what he was doing so he could watch.

"Wanna clue me in as to what you're looking for?" Recker asked.

"News is coming on."

"So?"

"I want to see how your exploits from earlier are covered," Jones said.

"Oh," Recker said, not seeming the least bit interested.

Though Jones always seemed to care how the media painted The Silencer, or what they said about him, Recker never seemed to care one way or the other. He figured no matter what they said, it wouldn't change what he did or how he operated. Regardless of anything they ever said about him, it never bothered him if they said something bad, or made him feel better if they heaped praise, so what was the point in listening?

"Why do you bother with that stuff?" Recker asked.

"It never hurts to be informed."

"You already are. I informed you about it earlier."

Within a few minutes, the two scenes where Recker left the dead bodies flashed across the screen, drawing Jones' attention even closer. Mia also stopped what she was doing and got up, moving to the couch. Recker sighed, knowing no more work was getting done for the moment since everyone seemed to be more focused on the TV. Jones turned up the volume so they could hear the reporter speak.

"Earlier today, spurred on by a 911 call, police arrived at this scene," the reporter said, looking and pointing back to the former auto garage. "Inside, they found the bodies of four men, all of whom have direct gang ties, and were pronounced dead at the scene. It is not believed the 911 call came from any of the dead men, and may have been the shooter. Though the motive of the shooting remains unclear at this time, there is a report The Silencer may have been involved, though that is unsubstantiated at this time."

The reporter then turned it over to another reporter

who was at the row home in West Philly. Jones looked over at Recker, who still seemed underwhelmed with everything and simply shrugged back at him.

"And we're here in West Philadelphia at this row home," the man said, turning toward the house. "The second major shooting of the day occurred here just a couple of hours after the one on sixty-second street, and also involved gang members. Police arrived at the boarded-up home, which appears to be a place where they conducted business activity inside, and found the bodies of four more gang related men, three of whom were found on the porch. There's no immediate word from the police on a possible motive, but nearby witnesses reported seeing a man walk out of the home immediately after the shooting. He was wearing a trench coat, and according to those witnesses, bore a striking resemblance to the man the media, and public, have affectionately called The Silencer. I should also point out another person was seen running from the house after the shooting, before The Silencer came out, if it was him, and witnesses have described this person as a kid, most likely a teenager. Theories abound within the neighborhood that The Silencer didn't want to shoot a kid and showed mercy on him by letting him leave unharmed."

"At least they threw in the good part," Recker said with a smile.

"So, to summarize, two crime scenes, a couple hours apart, eight men killed with gang ties, to the same gang it should be pointed out, and it appears... I stress appears, to be the work of The Silencer, though there is no official word that is the case," the reporter said, smiling, almost looking happy about it. "And we'll throw it back to you, Jim. The Silencer, he's out and about and looking like a one-man task force."

Nobody said another word as Jones got up and turned the TV off. For the amount of damage Recker inflicted, it was about as positive a news report as they could've made. It almost made him out to be a hero. No major surprise though, as the media and newspapers had usually talked about him in a positive way. There were only a few news anchors or reporters who talked of him as a negative for the city. Most seemed to enjoy covering stories The Silencer was reported to be involved in. He was kind of like a modern-day Robin Hood, only he wasn't stealing money for the poor. Instead, he was defending the innocent and killing the guilty.

"A one-man task force," Jones said, though not to anyone in particular as he walked back to the couch.

"You almost sound disappointed," Recker said. "Would you have rather they called me the face of evil? Or maybe the devil reincarnated?"

"On the contrary, it was a most enjoyable telecast of your exploits. Almost clapping at your daring escapades. Seemed the only thing missing was the standing ovation."

"Then why do you seem so annoyed by it? You almost seem like you would have wished they tore me apart or something."

"No, it's not that. I don't even know if I can quantify the meaning behind it. It just seems like they're beginning to glorify you. It's almost as if the reasons behind the killings don't matter, or the fact people are being hurt or killed, it's almost like it's the backstory. The headline is The Silencer strikes again."

"They're just doing what they have to do to sell newspapers, get subscribers, gain viewers," Recker said. "You know that as well as I do."

"I know. Is what you're doing important? Yes. Is killing sometimes necessary? Absolutely. It just seems wrong to glorify it."

Recker shrugged, thinking this was one of those times where Jones was taking it too far. "It is what it is. This is why I don't, and you shouldn't, care about listening to what others say. It makes no difference in the grand scheme of things."

"I guess you're right."

The trio went back to work for another hour before calling it a night. They had a lot of work to do and it'd already been a long day, especially for Recker. They figured getting some rest and coming back in the morning with a fresh pair of eyes and renewed energy would be just what the doctor ordered. They knew finding Jeremiah within any of the security footage they were going through was going to take some time. It was possible they could hit the mother lode quickly, but they all knew it wasn't the likely scenario. And it would turn out to be true.

A couple more days passed by without any new leads on Jeremiah's whereabouts. They got beeped a few times on the software program they were running, but every possibility the system brought up turned out to be a false hit. As another night wound down, Recker excused himself from the computer and went over to the coffee machine. He was quickly followed by Mia, who sensed Recker wasn't quite himself. She thought the lack of progress over finding Jeremiah might have been getting to him as he seemed more reserved than usual.

"You OK?" she asked, putting her hand on his back.

Recker looked at her and smiled, trying to put on a more positive face. "Yeah."

"You've been quieter today."

"Just tired I guess."

"You know you can talk to me if you need to."

"I know."

"So, what's bugging you?"

Recker looked down at his cup of coffee, stirring it around as he debated whether he wanted to pour out his feelings, which wasn't something he was fond of doing. "I guess I'm just a little mad at myself for allowing this to happen."

"Allow what to happen?"

"You being here."

"You don't want me here?" Mia asked, thinking he may have changed his mind about being with her.

"I want you to be able to enjoy your life. You've been here what, three or four days now?"

"I'm not complaining."

"That's because you're a good person. But the reality is, bad things have happened to you ever since you met me. You've been kidnapped twice, held hostage, almost killed, now there's another death threat on your head... and it's all because of me."

"Not entirely true."

"Which part?"

"Well, it's not all because of you," Mia said, trying to make light of things. "The one time was my fault for trying to be an investigator. You weren't even here for that one."

Recker looked at her and laughed, acknowledging her point. "Still, even so, you're here right now because you were seen sitting with me in a lunchroom."

"And I wouldn't change it. None of it. None of us know how things will turn out, Mike. We just make the best decisions we can and hope for the best. But it's not your fault."

"How you figure?"

"Because you told me numerous times how dangerous it was to be seen with you or be with you. I've always known that. Doing what you do, the people you know, I know sometimes there are risks, and I know sometimes there are consequences. It's not your fault. It's my choice. I understand as much. You never misled me, you never told me something just to keep me around, it was what I wanted to do. And if being here right now is a byproduct of that, then so be it. I wouldn't change it. As long as you're always here to protect me."

"You know I will," Recker whispered, leaning towards her

14

———

Six more days passed by, with still no sign of Jeremiah in any of the security camera footage they combed through. Frustrations were mounting, Recker the most, but even Jones and Mia were beginning to show signs of it. Though Mia tried to remain strong, as much as she could, being locked in an office for ten days without being able to go outside was starting to take a toll on her. She tried not to show it for Recker's sake, as she knew that him seeing her stressed would only serve to aggravate his own emotions further. He already blamed himself for most of what was happening, she didn't want to add fuel to his fire. After another unsuccessful day of searching, they were about to wrap things up for the night when Recker's phone rang. Whenever Vincent called personally, Recker knew it was something big.

"Hey," Recker said.

"It's a beautiful night out, isn't it?"

"I dunno. I haven't seen much of it. I'd say it's just fair."

"Well, the news I'm about to spring on you might brighten it for you," Vincent said.

"Which is?"

"First, I'd like to apologize for the length of time it's taken us to wrap up our end of the agreement. I must say he was quite elusive, much more than we initially gave him credit for. You were right, he was a slippery little guy."

"Bernal," Recker said.

"Yes. He's no longer a worry for anybody."

"You found him?"

"He's been... neutralized."

"You mean he's dead?"

"Well, I don't want to spoil things for you," Vincent said. "But I do believe if you catch the news in a few minutes, they may have something of interest for you."

"Oh? Like what?"

"As I said, I don't want to spoil things. I'll be in touch."

As Vincent hung up, Recker let the phone drop to his side, a look of confusion on his face. Jones could see whatever was said in the conversation was clearly perplexing to Recker. He just stood there for a minute, not moving in any way, deep in thought.

"Something troubling?" Jones asked.

"It was Vincent," Recker said.

"And?"

"And I don't know."

"Well what did he say?"

"Something about Bernal," Recker said, finally moving from his frozen stance.

"Is he dead?"

"I don't know. He wouldn't say. He just said he was neutralized."

"Well that could mean any number of things," Jones said.

"He said to turn on the news and there'd be something interesting on it."

"Well I guess we have to watch now."

Jones walked over to the TV and turned it on as the three of them sat down, greatly anticipating what was about to be shown. Even though Recker usually detested watching the news for his own exploits, he was eager to see what Vincent was talking about, especially since he wasn't involved in it. As the news telecast came on, nobody said a word as they all were focused on the contents of the show. After a few minutes, they came to what Vincent was referring to. A female reporter appeared on the screen with what was described as an explosive story.

"And it was a wild scene down here on North Eleventh Street as the body of a man who has since been identified as Adrian Bernal was found in the parking lot of the police department. The bullet-ridden body was discovered by officers of the sixth district several hours ago, and though the investigation into his death is still in its infancy, it's been learned Bernal was looking to kill one of the police officers in this district. We have also learned the police believe Bernal's killer to be The Silencer. Now, police are not divulging how or why they believe this is the work of The Silencer, but say they do have evidence suggesting it to be the case. We have talked to several officers off the record who have stated they believe The Silencer targeted Bernal in order to save one of their own, and for that, these officers expressed their gratitude to him."

As the reporter threw it back to the anchor desk, Jones turned off the TV after seeing all they needed to see. Recker continued staring at the television, even after it had been turned off. He was trying to think of why Vincent would want to prop him up like he just did. He could have gotten rid of Bernal easily and quietly, without any fanfare, but instead, Vincent chose to make Recker the hero of the story for some reason. Vincent definitely had a reason for doing so, he didn't do it out of the goodness of his heart, or because he felt like being a good guy. There was a business reason behind it. Something which would benefit him in the long run. Finally, after a few minutes, Mia spoke up to break the silence.

"Am I missing something?" she asked. "I don't get it. Why do they think it was you?"

"Because Vincent wanted it to be that way," Jones said.

"But why?"

"He's obviously after something."

Recker listened to them talking, while also trying to recollect every conversation he ever had with Vincent, before speaking up himself. "Before I took out Bellomi, Vincent told me he had people inside the police department on the payroll."

"So why not just give them the credit?" Mia said.

"Because he needs me to look good for something."

"For what purpose?" Jones said. "That's the question. And it's obviously something big."

Recker wasn't in the mood to debate it for the rest of the night, or spend the next few days wondering what Vincent had in mind. He already had enough on his mind. He didn't need more problems stirring around in his head. He immediately grabbed his phone and dialed Vincent's direct number. He didn't know if Vincent would pick up, but Recker wasn't going through Malloy for this one. He'd keep calling until Vincent answered. Somewhat surprisingly, Vincent answered after the first ring.

"I'm almost surprised it took this long for the phone to ring," Vincent said

"What was that about?"

"I figured you could use some goodwill amongst the police department."

"I don't need goodwill," Recker said.

"Well, maybe not, but you're the one who actually thwarted the plot Bernal was hatching. We were just the instrument that finished the job. But without your intel and guidance, it wouldn't have been possible. So, take the bow."

"I don't take bows. I don't do this for personal glory or headlines."

"Yes, I know. But having some friends within the police department can at times be a useful thing to have," Vincent said.

"I don't need friends."

"Oh, come now Mike, we all need friends. Sometimes it takes all kinds to be able to do the things that men like us do. Friends are willing to help you do things when a helping hand is needed."

Recker knew there was a hidden meaning behind that, though he wasn't sure what it was. "What exactly is that supposed to mean?"

Vincent didn't respond and moved on to the next subject. "So, how's your search for Jeremiah coming?"

"It's coming," Recker said.

"I couldn't help but notice his name hasn't emerged in any of the obituary columns. It's been ten days now. I have to say I expected you to have things wrapped up by now."

"Yeah, after our last meeting, he seems to have gone underground."

"I had a feeling he would."

"Getting anxious to move into your new territory?"

"Well, let's just say I expected our agreement to be over by now."

"Well if you can find him for me, you let me know so I can execute my end of it."

"Maybe I'll do that," Vincent said. "If we get anything, I'll contact you. Remember what I said about friends, though, Mike. Especially inside the police department. You did them a favor by taking out someone who came close to eliminating one of their own. There may be some who are willing to return the favor."

Before Recker was able to quiz him further on his statement, Vincent hung up. Now, instead of getting the answers he sought, Recker was only left with more questions. It was obvious Vincent had something specific on his mind, but he wasn't willing to share exactly what it was yet. Annoyed and frustrated at the events, Recker tossed the phone down in disgust, drawing a look from both Jones and Mia, who could tell he wasn't pleased.

"I take it you didn't get the answers you were looking for," Jones said.

"Not only did I not get the answers I was looking for, I didn't get any answers period. He gave me even more questions."

"What did he say?" Mia asked.

"He made a point to let me know how having friends in the police department was a good idea," Recker said, recalling the words vividly. "And he said by me doing a favor for them, maybe some of them would want to return the favor for me."

"What does that even mean?"

"Well, considering he has men inside the police, or at least on his payroll, he thinks somehow I can use them to my advantage in order to find Jeremiah."

"Even if that were true, finding the officer who was sympathetic to our cause and be willing to help, would not be an easy task in itself," Jones said.

"Unless we find the one who's on Vincent's payroll," Recker said.

They deliberated the merits of finding an ally on the police force, as Vincent seemed to suggest, for most of the rest of the night, eventually coming to the conclusion they weren't willing to go in that direction yet. They would rather keep on with what they were doing, going through the security footage, in the hopes of locating Jeremiah. At least for now. Recker was probably the one most interested in doing things Vincent's way. In his mind, it'd already taken longer than he wanted. He wanted it to be over now so Mia could get on with her life. And so could he. He was more willing to make a deal, if it meant getting rid of Jeremiah once and for all. Jones and Mia were the ones more interested in staying the course, even if it meant it took longer. But even though Recker was for it, he allowed the others to sway his opinion, at least for the time being.

Unfortunately, five more days passed, and they were no closer to finding Jeremiah than they were when they started. After Recker took out two of his properties and a bunch of his men, Jeremiah went completely into hiding. Though he usually visited one or two nightclubs a week over the past several years, he hadn't even done that. So even if Recker and Jones had found footage of him somewhere, it wouldn't have done them any good. Jeremiah wouldn't be showing up, anyway. By then, everyone was getting frustrated, and it was starting to show, though it showed the worst on Recker. With all of them working at a computer, Recker had enough. He thought it was getting them nowhere, and he'd had enough. He pounded his fist on the desk and angrily pushed his chair away, standing up and walking over to the window, looking down at the parking lot. Jones and Mia looked at each other, both of whom were leery of going over and talking to him. Eventually, Jones was the one who spoke up.

"Michael."

Recker spun around, anger seething off his tongue. "This isn't working, David. It's not working," he said loudly. "We've been at this for two weeks and we're still nowhere. We're not any closer to finding him."

"We knew it would take some time," Jones said. "To think we were going to get someone like Jeremiah in a matter of days was not a realistic time frame."

"OK. You're right. But we're not at a few days now. Yesterday was fourteen days. She can't sit in here forever," Recker said, pointing at Mia.

"Mike, I'm fine," Mia said, trying to diffuse his temper.

"But I'm not," he said, in a more soothing manner. "You can't live like this anymore."

"Honestly, I haven't really minded. I've been with you more these last couple weeks than in the past two years. I've enjoyed being close to you."

Recker tried to muster a smile, though he barely showed it. "I just want this to be over."

"We all do," Jones said. "But we can't force something which isn't there."

"But we can. And we both know what I'm talking about."

"Vincent."

Recker shrugged, "I'm ready."

"And what do you think will come out of this? Another deal with Vincent?"

"It's the same deal," Recker said. "I'm getting Jeremiah. I just need his help locating him."

"And you don't think it will come with an additional cost?"

"Does it matter at this point? Vincent will get what he wants, control of the city. That's all he needs."

Jones clasped his hands together and rested them against his forehead as he put his elbows on the desk, looking down as he collected his thoughts. Deep down, he knew Recker was probably right. They were having a tough time finding Jeremiah, much tougher than Jones thought they would. He just hated the idea of going to Vincent again. Though the two sides always seemed to align with each other up to then, Jones didn't like working so closely with them. After all, they were on different sides of the fence. Though Vincent sometimes helped them achieve their goals, at heart, he was still the boss of a major criminal organization which was slowly taking control of the city. That was always worrisome to Jones. But he looked over at Mia, thinking of her being cooped up in there for the last two weeks, and not making a sound. She never made one complaint, not one argument, and if she was ever frustrated, he never noticed it. No matter his feelings for Vincent or the situation, Jones felt they owed it to her to get it resolved. The quicker the better. He looked back at Recker and nodded, ready to give his blessing.

"You're right. It's time," Jones said.

Recker nodded back, taking a final look out the window before calling Vincent. "You know, I know we've talked before about this, but I can't help but think somehow, he's manipulated me this entire time."

"How so?"

"Taking out Bellomi. Now Jeremiah."

"We've been over this. You've done what was necessary."

"I know. But do you ever think he's orchestrated things, pushed things in a certain direction, to get things just right, to get things into a position where I'd have to respond the way I do?"

Jones shook his head, not having an answer. "Unfortunately, that's something I don't think we'll ever know. It's one of the reasons I hate being involved with him. Because we both know he's capable of things like that."

Recker then called Vincent, getting him immediately.

"Mike, what can I do for you?" he said.

Recker hesitated, almost afraid to say he needed help again. "I'm uh... I guess I'm ready to make some friends."

He could almost hear Vincent smiling through the phone. "Well, it's nice to hear it. Took a little longer than I anticipated, but nonetheless, still nice to hear."

"I can't find him." Recker sighed. "I've been looking nonstop and I just don't know where he is."

"I do."

"What?"

"I know where he is."

"You do? How?" Recker asked, surprised.

"I've always known. Don't forget, Mike, information is my business. I collect information like some people collect trading cards. It pours into me by the truckloads."

"Well if you've known, then why haven't you taken him out yourself?"

Vincent laughed, like he thought it was a ridiculous question. "Because it wasn't our deal, was it?"

"No."

"So, what do you need from me?"

"Just tell me where he's at. I'll get him," Recker said.

"Well, that's a little easier said than done. He's got at least ten to fifteen men with him."

"So, what do you propose then?"

"Remember what I said about friends, Mike. Let them help."

"And just what friends do you keep referring to?"

"It'll take some faith on your part," Vincent said.

"In what?"

"In me. Do you have it?"

"Yes."

"Good. Here is the plan then. Jeremiah has holed himself up in a house on the west side. As I mentioned, he's got men with him. At nine o'clock tonight, a small team of police officers will converge on the building. You will be among them."

"And do they know this?"

"Remember what I said about friends, Mike. You did them a favor by protecting one of their own. They would like to return the favor by helping you."

"And after it's done, they're just gonna let me walk out of there?" Recker asked.

"Faith, Mike, faith."

"OK. Even if I go along with this, if they converge on the building, why wouldn't they just kill Jeremiah themselves? What am I needed for?"

"Well, unfortunately in this day and age, the police

aren't trusted as much as the olden days. Not with body cameras and the like," Vincent said.

"And? I know there's more."

"I want Jeremiah dead. Him in prison just means I'll have to deal with him again at some point, or men who are still loyal to him. But if he's dead, I don't have that problem."

"No argument from me there," Recker said.

"So, the officers converging on this building tonight may be on my payroll, but they're still police officers, not a death squad. If it turns out that Jeremiah is killed in a firefight as they storm the building, then there's no issue. They'd have done their job."

"And if Jeremiah doesn't put up a fight?"

"Well, that's something that we just can't have, can we?" Vincent asked.

"That's where I come in."

"Exactly. I can't have police officers executing an unarmed man, one who's given up, and have it on camera. That's an officer I'd end up losing."

"But I don't have a camera," Recker said, understanding the plan. "But aren't they gonna see me on camera?"

"Well, you know how technology is. It's a fickle thing. Two of the officers will have a problem with their cameras for a few minutes. They'll go offline long enough to do what needs to be done."

"So, I'm there as backup?"

"If they decide to fight and die, you can sit this one

out. If they give up for another day, well, you'll be there to make sure that day never arrives," Vincent said.

"One more question, what do you need me for? You could have Malloy do that. He's just as willing and capable."

"Well, you know the old risk versus reward. If in the unlikely chance that something goes wrong, someone escapes, someone's identified, I can't have someone from my organization knowingly involved."

"But I'm a known independent."

"Exactly."

"So, who do I report to tonight?"

"Detective Nix. He's leading the team. He'll be apprised of the plan."

"And he'll be OK with it?"

"Faith, Mike, faith."

As they finished their talk, Recker put the phone back in his pocket and continued looking out the window. Jones was listening in to the conversation as much as possible, trying to piece together what he could from Recker's end of it. He didn't quite like what he heard.

"Would you like to fill us in?" Jones asked. "Because I'm pretty sure some of what you were saying sounded troubling."

Recker turned around and informed Jones and Mia of the plan. Mia seemed OK with it. She certainly wasn't going to go against Recker's wishes, and if he thought this was the best way to get it done, she'd go along with it. Jones, though, he wasn't so sure. Not only were they aligning with Vincent, but they had to put their faith in him, hoping the police officers wouldn't arrest Recker after he killed Jeremiah. Vincent could get rid of Jeremiah, and Recker, in a few short minutes.

"I'm aware of the risks, David," Recker said.

"But you're willing to take them, anyway?"

"I have to believe Vincent doesn't want to get rid of me right now."

"Why are you so willing to think that?" Jones asked.

"Because we're not enemies."

"It doesn't mean you're not a threat to him. All his enemies will be gone. He may think you're the next one."

Recker took a few minutes to think about it, but his mind was made up. It was something he couldn't pass up, regardless of the risks. "I have to do this."

Jones still had his reservations, but he knew he was unlikely to talk Recker out of it. Recker spent the rest of the night mentally preparing himself for what was about to happen, trying to go over all the possibilities he could face. He was texted the address, and while Jones had the idea of going there without help, Recker quickly shot the idea down. If Jeremiah had ten to fifteen men with him, even for a man like Recker, it'd be tough for him to get past everyone. Once eight o'clock hit, Recker started getting himself ready, checking his guns. Jones and Mia had walked closer to the door to see him off.

"Just be careful," Jones said, shaking Recker's hand.

"I will."

Mia reached up and kissed Recker passionately on the lips. "Just make sure you come back to me."

"Nothing will stop me from doing that," Recker said, giving her a smile.

Recker arrived at the house in question at 8:45. The police officers had already surrounded the end unit row home. Unlike the other properties that Jeremiah had, this one wasn't boarded-up. It looked like a perfectly normal home that any family would live in. Nothing to suggest that a dangerous criminal was inside with a bunch of his thugs. As Recker walked down the sidewalk, past the metal fence, a police officer was near the gate and looked back at him, seeing him approach.

"Are you him?" the officer asked. "You're The Silencer?"

Recker nodded. "That's me."

"I'm Detective Nix," he said, sticking his hand out.

Recker was a bit surprised, but he returned the handshake.

"We're just about ready to go in," Nix said.

"What do you need from me?"

"Nothing yet. The team will go in first. They'll clear everything. If you're needed, I'll let you know."

"And if I'm not, you're just gonna let me walk out of here?" Recker asked, still having doubts.

"Listen, some of us wanna lock you up. Some of us think you're doing good by the city and us."

"And where do you stand?"

"You saved one of us from biting the bullet," Nix said. "For me, you get a free ride. Even if you hadn't, every jerk you take out, is one more that I don't have to worry about. So, for me, as long as you're taking out the bad guys, we're on the same side as far as I'm concerned."

"Good to know."

"We're good to go," a voice said over the radio.

"All right, everyone go!" Nix commanded.

The officers went through both the front and back door, and within seconds, massive amounts of gunfire erupted. Recker and Nix stood there by the front gate, looking on and listening. It was an unusual stance for Recker, as he was usually the one doing the shooting. It felt weird that he was watching the activities unfold, waiting for someone else to do the dirty work. Felt even more strange that he was standing next to a police officer, who wasn't lifting a finger against him. Though it seemed like the battle was raging on forever, it was actually only about ten minutes. After that, voices started crackling over the radio.

"We'll be coming out in a minute," an officer said.

"What's everyone's status?" Nix asked.

"One officer wounded, shot in the arm, he'll be OK. No casualties on our end."

"Good. What about our targets?"

"Six dead. Four in custody. We'll be bringing them out."

"And the main one?" Nix asked, not wanting to mention his name over the air.

"He's locked in a room. I've got a man on it."

"All right, bring the others out. I'll send the package in."

"Ten-four."

Nix looked over at Recker and nodded. "Looks like you're up."

"OK."

Recker started to walk to the house but was interrupted by the detective. "Hey, when it's done, just slip out the back door."

"Thanks."

Nix nodded at him in appreciation. As Recker reached the front door, he was met by another officer. "Hey," the officer said. "My camera's gonna be out for about sixty seconds. I'll get you to the room then the rest is up to you."

"Got it."

The officer led Recker to the basement, which had been divided into a couple of rooms. There was another officer standing by the door to make sure Jeremiah didn't escape. He was given the nod to go away, which he complied with.

"Does he have a weapon in there?" Recker asked.

"Can't say for sure," the officer said. "He was seen retreating in there without anything in his hands. He locked the door once he got in there. Whether he's got anything stashed in there, we're not sure."

"OK."

"Thanks for all you do," the officer who led Recker there said, giving him a pat on the shoulder before leaving himself.

It all seemed very strange to Recker, getting what amounted to a police escort inside the building. He was getting patted on the back and words of appreciation, it almost seemed like a dream. He got out his gun and tried to think of how he'd handle it. He could just kick the door in and rush Jeremiah, but he didn't want to walk into a bullet either. He thought if Jeremiah knew it was him on the other side, maybe he'd react differently than if it was the police.

"Jeremiah," Recker yelled.

"Recker?" Jeremiah shouted back.

"Police are gone. It's just you and me."

"How'd you manage that one?"

"Guess it pays to know people."

"Yeah. Guess it does."

"You know why I'm here. Why don't you come out and get it over with?" Recker asked.

"Why don't you come in and get me?"

With his defiant tone, Recker got the feeling Jeremiah was armed in the room. Maybe he was just stalling the inevitable as long as possible, but Recker wouldn't take the chance of thinking he didn't have a gun and wind up taking a bullet himself. After looking around for a second, Recker didn't see anything else he could use. He also knew with the police in front, he didn't have a lot of time. Though they seemed to be giving him a pass out of there, he didn't want to take advantage for too long.

He took a few steps back, then violently kicked the door open, keeping mind to stay out of view. As soon as it flung open, bullets ripped into the door, as Recker took cover to the side of it. He peeked his head around to get a view of the layout. As he did, another shot rang out, a bullet whizzing past his head, just missing. There didn't appear to be much furniture in the room. It looked like just a couch and a table, along with a TV. Recker took another peek inside, and without any gunshots coming toward him, rushed inside. He dropped to the ground and waited for Jeremiah to emerge from behind the couch. As Jeremiah rose up to fire again, Recker unloaded four shots in quick succession, knocked his victim back against the wall, his gun flying out of his hand. After Jeremiah banged against the wall, he dropped to the floor. Recker quickly got up and rushed around the couch to his position, ready to finish him off if necessary. Jeremiah was just lying there, not moving, as blood poured out of his body from the four bullets lodged in his chest. Recker stood over him and shook his head, thinking it didn't have to end up that way. If Jeremiah hadn't taken the steps he did, they never would have had to become enemies. But it wasn't something Recker would worry over too much.

Just as Detective Nix suggested, Recker didn't waste any time stewing around, and took off through the back door. Though he didn't feel any uneasiness, he was still ready for anything, in the event he was double crossed. Luckily, everyone involved kept their word. Recker immediately went back to the office. Although he assumed Vincent would find out from his officers, Recker called him on the way back, just to let him know everything went according to plan. When he finally got back to the office, Jones and Mia were at one of the desks, looking like they were praying. They had their elbows on the table, and their hands folded together, resting against their faces. But once they heard the door jiggling, they rushed over to it, happy to see Recker returning. Mia almost knocked him over as she jumped into his arms, giving him a kiss and some much-needed affection. Jones shook his hand, also excited to see him return.

"Don't expect a kiss from me," Jones said.

"Don't worry, this is the only one I need," Recker said, wrapping his arms fully around Mia.

DOUBLE TAP PREVIEW

Please enjoy the following 3 Chapter preview of the next book in The Silencer Series, Double Tap.

15

CHAPTER 1

Recker looked completely uncomfortable. There was no question he was out of his element. It was a day he knew was coming for weeks, and he wasn't looking forward to it at all. But he knew it was one of the give-and-takes that he had to do if he wanted Mia to remain part of his life. After three months of talking and deliberating, they finally decided on a place to live together. His apartment. His bare walls, his scant furniture, the barely livable arrangements, they were all about to go. Replaced by pictures, more comfortable surroundings, and things that smelled nice. And he wasn't all that warm and fuzzy about it.

"A little to the left," Mia said.

Recker closed his eyes and sighed, thinking if anyone saw him now, his reputation would take a severe hit. Well, maybe not severe, but he'd sure have to put up with a lot of ribbing and good-natured abuse. After all, hanging curtains wasn't exactly something anyone would ever expect to see him doing. He certainly never thought so. But, it was the price he had to pay to be with the woman that he cared about. As long as nobody saw him do the homely duties.

"One day I'm shooting people and the next I'm hanging curtains," Recker mumbled to himself. "Unreal."

"What, honey?"

"Uh, nothing. Which way you want these?"

Though Jeremiah and his gang were now out of the picture, Recker didn't want Mia staying in her former apartment. He'd actually pleaded with her to quit her job and stay at home, that way he could be sure nobody would ever try taking advantage of her again. But that flew on deaf ears. Though Mia loved and wanted to be with him, she wasn't going to stash herself away and become a vegetable. She loved her job; she loved helping people, and she was determined to keep doing just that.

Recker still had concerns, but knew it was a lost cause in trying to change her mind. It just wouldn't happen. So he did the next best thing. He taught her how to be elusive. How to become invisible. And it wasn't just for her safety, but also for his. Nobody knew where he lived other than Jones. The last thing Recker needed was somebody following her and finding out where his home was. So they agreed that she would never drive straight home to the apartment after work. She would take a few extra turns to make sure there was nobody in her rear-view mirror. Recker taught her which ways to go, and also how to spot if someone was tailing her. Over the previous month, he rigged up some practice situations where he used a different car to teach her how to, not only spot someone following her, but also how to escape them. After a month of practice, Mia had gotten relatively good at the practice. She'd never be at a CIA level of elusiveness, but she wasn't half-bad. He figured if anyone ever attempted to follow her after that point, they'd most likely not be as good as he was. And if they were, they'd most likely find him eventually, anyway. She was at least good enough to satisfy Recker's worries for the time being. In any case, he'd continue working with her to sharpen her skills in the event she ever had to put them into use, which hopefully she wouldn't.

Once the curtains had been hung to Mia's satisfaction, Recker stared out the window for a few moments. As he was daydreaming, Mia continued unpacking some of her things, as well as some new things she'd bought for the apartment. Recker's gaze was interrupted as he noticed Mia putting some small, potted plants on the windowsill. He looked at her with a curious expression, almost like he wasn't sure what she was doing.

"What's that?" Recker said.

"Uh, plants."

"Why are you putting them there?"

"To decorate the apartment?" Mia replied, sensing that he was skeptical of her arrangements.

"Oh."

"Would you like me to take them down?"

"No. No. It's fine," Recker said, though he really did have some reservations about it.

"Are you sure?"

He tried to make a face to indicate he had no issues, though not very well. "Totally."

Mia smiled at him, thinking it was cute how he had hang-ups over a few small plants. "It'll be OK," she said, patting his shoulder reassuringly.

"I'm fine. It's just I've never actually had plants before."

"Don't worry about them. I'll take care of them."

"Good. Cause I'm good at killing things. Plants probably included."

Mia laughed and gave him a pat on the shoulder as she went back to some of the boxes that were littered along the floor. He turned around just in time to see the horror of her taking out a few pictures that were already in frames. He stood there dumbfounded, his mouth slightly open, as he watched her nail the frames to the wall. There were some pictures of her, some of him, and some of them together.

"I need a case," Recker whispered. "I'm not made for this."

After putting a few pictures up, Mia turned around to grab another one when she noticed the blank expression on his face. Though she was amused at how uncomfortable the simplest of things seemed to make him, she tried to be understanding and not show it. She knew the barren landscape of the apartment before she got there was likely how his places had looked for the past ten years or so. It was probably all he ever knew. She walked over to him with a sad puppy dog kind of a smile and put her arms around him to give him a kiss, trying to be as sympathetic as possible. Though Mia was enjoying herself immensely, she knew it was hard for him. Change wasn't something that Recker was accustomed to or liked very much.

"It's going to be OK," she said. "I promise."

Her affection briefly helped to alleviate his anxiety over his changing life. A warm look into her eyes was enough to ease the fears of any man, Recker included. There was just something about the way she looked at him that made him feel more secure in his changing environment. At least when her arms were wrapped around him.

"When did you do all that?" Recker said, not aware that she ever had pictures of them made.

"Well, the pictures of us were the selfies I took of us. And the ones of just you were just pics that I took randomly. You've seen them before."

"I know. I just didn't realize that you printed them out."

"Is that a problem?" she said with a smile.

"No. It just makes things seem... permanent."

"I can take them down if it makes you uncomfortable."

"No, it's fine. I'm just... not used to looking at myself on the wall," Recker said.

Seeing the pictures of them together on the wall was a little jarring to him. In his mind, it was like a symbol of their relationship cementing. And though he still wasn't as comfortable with it as he tried to pretend he was, he knew Mia would be crushed if she had to take them down because of his uneasiness. It was just something he'd have to deal with.

Once Mia went back to hanging more pictures, Recker started feeling uneasy again. He started to think that maybe he just needed to get out of the apartment for a while. Maybe it was just the process of seeing all the changes unfold in front of his eyes that fueled his anxiety. Maybe if he went out and everything was done once he got back, he would feel much better about the situation. He thought maybe it wasn't the actual changes themselves that was causing his worries, and if everything was already done, it wouldn't bother him as much.

Recker pulled out his phone, praying that Jones had tried to call or text him. Even though he knew Jones hadn't, he hoped that somehow, he just missed the call. Maybe he didn't hear the ringer as Mia was talking to him about something. Or maybe he missed a text message when he was in a trance over what seemed like a strange apartment to him. But as Recker checked, his hopes were quickly dashed. There were no calls. No texts. But as he continued to watch Mia alter his apartment, or as he needed to get used to saying, their apartment, he knew he needed to escape for a while. Seeing he was supposed to have the day off, Mia was a little concerned when she noticed him looking at his phone.

"Everything OK?" Mia said.

"Oh. Uh, yeah. Yeah, everything's fine."

"Then why are you looking at your phone like that?"

"It's uh... it's David," Recker said, quickly thinking of something. "Yeah. He just texted me about something. I should probably call him back to see what's up."

"You were supposed to be with me all day," she said,

disappointed about what she suspected was about to happen.

"Well, let me just see what he wants. Maybe it's not what you think."

Recker walked into the kitchen as he called Jones' number, hoping that the professor had somehow come up with a new case. The actual move-in day for Mia had already been postponed a couple of times when newer, more urgent types of cases had unexpectedly popped up at the last minute. Jones had personally assured her the previous day that nothing was on the horizon.

"David, I saw you called, what's up?"

"Um... what?" Jones said.

"So what's going on?"

"Nothing's going on. What call? I didn't call you."

"Oh. Well is it serious?"

"Serious? What are you talking about? Is everything all right there?"

"Yeah, everything's going fine here."

"I'm glad to hear it."

"So you really think you need me?" Recker said.

"Are we back to this again? What are you talking about?"

"Yeah, I suppose I can be down there in a while if you really think it's necessary."

"Michael, nothing is going on."

"She'll be disappointed, but she'll understand."

"Do we have a bad connection or something?" Jones said, looking at his phone in bewilderment.

"I can leave in about five minutes."

"Leave for what?"

"All right. I'll see you when I get there," Recker said, hanging up.

Jones sat there for a minute, trying to figure out what had just happened. He continued staring at his phone, lying on the desk. "I hope he hasn't gone crazy after less than one day of being domesticated."

Before going back into the living room, Recker looked at kitchen cabinets and let out a sigh. He wasn't that proud of himself for what he was about to do, deceiving Mia like he was. But he figured on the importance level as far as lies go, this one would rank on the bottom of the list. As he thought about it for a few more moments, he actually convinced himself it was better this way, anyway. Interior decorating wasn't his thing, and there wasn't much he could add. The only thing he could really do was get in the way. Mia would probably be better off, or at least faster, if she didn't have to stop every few minutes to massage his feelings over his changing apartment.

When Recker finally came back in, Mia didn't need him to say anything. She'd already overheard his conversation with Jones. Recker had made sure that he talked loud enough for her to hear. By the look on her face, he could tell that she wasn't pleased. She was just standing there looking at him, a picture frame in each hand, which were dropped down on each side of her by her knees. Recker started to open her mouth to explain before she stopped him. She lifted her left index finger off the frame and held it out in front of her, so he didn't say a word.

"I know," she sighed in frustration, yet still somehow mustering a smile. "You've gotta go."

"I'm sorry. It's just that something's come up."

"I know. I know. Something always comes up."

Recker walked over to her to try to smooth over her frustrations. He put his hands on her waist and brought her closer to him, giving her a gentle kiss on the lips.

"Bribery will not get you anywhere," Mia said, though the kiss wiped away the look of displeasure on her face.

"Are you sure?" Recker said, kissing her again.

"Well..."

"Besides, you'll get all this done a lot faster if I'm not here. You know I'm not really helping here."

"I just wanted this to be a special moment for us."

Recker knew it was important for her and took a moment to look around the room. "This isn't what's special. These things are just... things. The only special moment I need is when you're like this, when you're in my arms."

"You're lucky you're so good looking," Mia said, kissing him again, as all her displeasure faded away.

"I think it'll be better this way, anyway. You'll be able to do things the way you want without having to constantly look over at me to see if I'm hyperventilating."

"But what if I do something that you don't like?"

"I'm sure that everything you do will be perfect," Recker said. "Besides, the thing that matters to me most is that you're here. Everything else I can get used to. It might take some time, but I'll get used to it... eventually."

After a few more minutes of affection, Recker finally

pulled himself away from Mia and went down to the office. And though she was initially disappointed at him leaving, she knew that everything would go by faster if he was gone. Not that her first priority was speed, but she didn't want to spend the whole day doing it either. When Recker got down to the office, about thirty minutes had elapsed since his phone call with Jones. Based on the strangeness of the conversation, the professor didn't know if Recker was actually coming or not. When he saw Recker enter the office, he stopped what he was doing and started peppering his partner with questions, wondering if he was losing his mind.

"Would you mind explaining what that phone call was about?" Jones said, getting up from his chair to greet his friend.

"Oh. I, uh, just needed to get away for awhile."

"Get away? Are you two already having compatibility problems on your first day of cohabitation?"

Recker thought for a moment. "What?"

Jones rolled his eyes, not believing that he didn't understand what he was talking about. "Are you two having issues already?"

"Oh. No. Nothing like that."

"Then why are you here? You both practically begged for a day off so you could fix up the apartment to suit both your tastes. And now you're saying you needed to get away?"

"Well, it's not a big deal," Recker said. "It's not like we're arguing or styles clashing or anything."

"Then what is it?"

"It's more or less me. I guess it's a little harder than I thought it'd be. Seeing everything transform from my way of doing things to a... more pleasant atmosphere will take some getting used to."

"Perhaps you're not as ready for this as you thought you were," Jones said.

"No, that's not it. I love her. I do. This is what I want. She's what I want. It's just... I've spent a lot of years doing things one way, my way. Not having to worry about what someone else would like or think."

"You'll adjust."

"I know. I just hope I don't drive her crazy in the process."

"Or me."

"So is there still nothing on the agenda?" Recker said.

"No. We're still clear."

Since he was there, and didn't have anywhere else to go, Recker sat down at the desk and went on the computer. He figured he'd just sit there for a couple hours doing busy work, trying to occupy some time before he went back home.

"So how long do you plan on continuing this little charade of yours and sitting here?" Jones said.

"I dunno. Two or three hours maybe. Why? Wanna get rid of me already?"

"No. Just wondering."

Jones also sat back down, though he had more definitive plans for his day. There were still a few cases that he was running down information on, but they were probably still a day or two away from acting on anything.

His main goal for the day was finishing up on something that he'd been hiding from Recker. It was nothing like the last secret he was hiding from him, about Agent 17. This time, he assumed Recker would be pleased. At least he hoped so. After all, it was Recker's idea.

Finding another agent to work within their little group was something they'd discussed previously, and Recker knew Jones had started doing some work on it, Jones never divulged his progress or indicated how close he really was. Jones altered his search methods somewhat this time, though. If there was anything that he learned from Recker's situation, it was that he didn't want to get another former agent who was in hot water. This time, Jones focused his efforts on finding ex-CIA agents who were no longer employed with the agency, but were still in good standing. That way they would never have to worry about being tracked or worry about being found. After an exhaustive search over the past several months, Jones finally targeted someone, firmly believing that he found his man.

Jones hadn't made any plans on when or how he'd tell Recker though. He figured it would be more of a feeling out process. Recker obviously wasn't good with change, and even though he initially seemed on board with the idea, Jones wasn't sure it'd be good to spring it on him now with the changes he had going on with Mia. But it was also something that he needed Recker's approval on. If they brought in someone new, it had to be someone they could both work with. Someone they had chemistry with. Especially Recker. If they were out in the field,

Recker had to feel comfortable that a new person would have his back. That he could trust him. That was no small feat. When it came time to calling on the new recruit, Jones wanted Recker to be there to get his thoughts. Recker was good with initial encounters, and getting a feel on how people were.

Jones decided he'd wait a few more days before talking to Recker about it. He just felt that now wasn't the best time to make Recker's life even more chaotic. He'd give Recker some time to adjust to living with Mia and being in what was basically a brand-new apartment. It was going to be tough for Jones, though, not to spill the beans on what he thought was an exciting development. The man that he tabbed for the next member of their crusade was someone that Jones felt would be a great addition to the team. Someone that wasn't all that different from Recker. Well, hopefully for Jones there'd be one small difference... that he didn't have the same appetite for violence.

CHAPTER 2

J ones waited another week before talking to Recker about the prospective new member of the team. He assumed that was long enough for Recker to get used to his surroundings. And if it wasn't, well, that was as long as Jones was giving him, anyway. With each day that passed, Recker seemed a little more comfortable with how things were going. He didn't seem as anxious or nervous about what was happening at home. Then, one morning when Recker came into the office, Jones figured it was time to clue him in on his activities.

"Everything going well in your new man cave?" Jones couldn't keep a playful smile from playing across his face.

"Don't get cute."

"I'm sorry. I just couldn't resist the temptation."

"Yeah, yeah."

"Drapes fastened, pictures hung?"

"You don't fasten drapes," Recker said.

"Oh. Well I see we are learning new skills, aren't we?" Jones said, continuing the teasing. "Now you even know the correct procedures on curtains. My, my. If your enemies could only see you now."

Recker rolled his eyes, then looked up at the ceiling, contorting his face to make it seem like he was mad, though he really wasn't. "Are you done now?"

"Yes, I think so."

"Are you sure? Anymore quips or jokes? Might as well get them out now."

"No, I believe I'm done."

Recker sat down at the desk to start working as Jones walked over to him to spill the big news. Jones grabbed a file folder off the desk containing all his information before he approached his partner. He wanted to tell him early, before they got too knee-deep into anything.

"So, you remember what we talked about a few months ago?" Jones said, sitting on the edge of the desk. "About adding another person to the team?"

"Yeah." Recker wasn't paying Jones much attention as he typed away on the computer.

"Well, I've been thinking more about it."

"Oh? Finally come around on it?"

"Well, in a way. You're sure you're good with it?"

"Of course. It was my idea if you remember," Recker said, still not looking at him. "I mean, I don't want to add just anybody. As long as they got the skills and a personality that we'll both get along with, then yeah, I'm still good with it."

"Then perhaps you should look at this." Jones held out the folder.

Getting the clue that Jones had more on his mind than he was saying, Recker finally stopped typing and looked at the professor. He glanced at the file folder, then took it out of his hands. Recker opened it, immediately seeing a picture and bio sheet of Christopher Haley. He intently looked it over for a few minutes before looking back up at Jones.

"This is the guy?" Recker said.

"Unless you have objections."

Recker turned his attention back to the contents of the folder. He read the bio sheet a couple of times before moving on to the other information that Jones had compiled on him. Jones had printed out everything he could find on Haley. Every case he worked on in the CIA, his life before he joined the government agency, and every detail since he'd left.

"Well, I'll let you read that without me looking over your shoulder." Jones walked around Recker and back to his own workstation.

Jones had probably compiled at least a hundred pages of information and notes on Haley. Not only the facts and details of Haley's life, but he had also added his own notes and thoughts. It was a meticulously prepared folder, something one would expect coming from him, bringing someone in to an operation such as the one they were running, one that would take Recker several hours to go over. Though Jones wasn't going to bug Recker about his thoughts until he was completely done consuming the file, he did keep an ear out, hoping to hear any sounds that Recker might make as he was reading. Maybe some grumbles if he didn't like something he read, or maybe something more lighthearted if he approved. Something that would give Jones an indication on which way Recker was leaning before they discussed it after he was done.

Unfortunately for Jones, Recker never gave any clues or hints on his thoughts as he was reading. He was stone-cold silent. And on something like this, Recker wasn't going to rush his way through. He was going to sit, read, and analyze. Possibly several times over. Jones knew he was going to be in for a long day. It occurred to him that maybe he should've given Recker the file toward the end of the day. That way he could've taken it home with him. Now, it was unlikely they were going to get any further work done. Luckily there was nothing pressing. After five hours of silence, without either man saying a word, or asking Recker a thing about his thoughts up to that point, Jones couldn't stand being left in the dark anymore. He needed some clarification about Recker's thoughts.

"So, what do you think?" Jones finally said.

"I'm still reading."

"I can see that. But surely you must have some thoughts at this point. Either one way or the other."

"Not yet."

"Come on, Mike. You've been reading for five hours. You don't have any inclination on which way you're leaning after five hours?"

"There's a lot to think about."

"Yes, I understand that. Does he at least seem promising?" Jones said, hoping to get even the littlest nugget of positive emotion out of Recker's mouth.

"Uh... maybe."

Jones sighed and scratched behind his ear, frustrated that Recker wasn't going to humor him and tell him a thing. Recker wasn't going to do this on his own timeline.

"Do you think you'll have an answer today?" Jones said.

"Maybe."

"Oh, good lord. You're not going to give me the slightest of hints about anything, are you?"

"We'll see."

Jones knew it was a lost cause at that point. Recker wasn't going to tell him anything. And based upon the fact that Recker seemed to be reading the pages repeatedly, and he still had a few to go, Jones thought it possible that Recker might not even be ready to give an opinion before the day was over.

"Should I order a late-night snack?" Jones said, only partly kidding.

"Not something we should rush through."

"I'm aware of that."

"Maybe I should take this home with me tonight," Recker said. "That way I can have an answer for you in the morning."

"You're really going to put me through all that agony?"

"Why not? You're a patient person."

"In most cases. This doesn't happen to be one of those times."

"Why? What's so special about this? You seem very anxious for some reason."

"What's so special about this? We're talking about adding a number to our twosome. I've spent months working on this, finding candidates, discarding candidates, until I finally whittled it down to one. This one. So yes, I am a little anxious about this."

"Well I need time to analyze this. I can't give my thumbs up until I've fully vetted everything in here."

"Don't you think I've done that? Do you really believe I'd come to you with this unless I was absolutely sure on this?"

"What do you want? You want me to just rubber-stamp this?" Recker said.

"Of course not."

"Then let me dig into it on my own. I know you're anxious about it. Just relax."

Jones knew he wasn't going to speed up Recker's analysis, so he tried to block it out the best he could. He turned back toward his computer and started working again on some of the upcoming cases they had. He needed to do something engrossing, so he could forget about Recker reading the mountain of information next to him. The only thing he could think of was working on another case. And it worked. Jones completely blocked Recker out of his mind for the next hour until Recker finally made a noise.

"Crap," Recker said, drawing a concerned look from Jones, who thought he'd read something that he didn't like.

"What's the matter? What don't you like?"

"Nothing," Recker said, getting up from his chair.

"Then what are you doing?"

"It's past six o'clock. I'm supposed to be off today. Remember, I've got a girlfriend redecorating my apartment."

"Oh. I almost forgot about that."

"Yeah, well, I don't wanna be gone all day and night. She forgave me for coming. I don't know if she'll forgive me for staying indefinitely."

"What about Mr. Haley?" Jones said.

"I'll take his file with me and read it tonight."

"I was hoping I'd get a yay or nay from you tonight."

"Not likely. I'll have an answer in the morning," Recker said.

Though Jones wasn't especially pleased with waiting another day, he knew that was the best he was going to get. As Recker grabbed the file folder and walked toward the door, Jones tried one last time to get some information out of him.

"You're seriously going to just leave like that? You're not even going to give me a hint as to which way you're leaning?"

Without saying a word, Recker looked back and gave Jones a sinister smile, realizing he was torturing his partner without saying anything.

"You know, you have a mean streak in you," Jones said.

"Consider it payment for your needling about the curtains," Recker said, closing the door behind him.

In reality, Recker was very impressed with the file that

Jones had accumulated on Haley. There were no obvious red flags that Recker could see. He spent eight years in the military, four of them in special forces, along with another eight years in the CIA doing clandestine operations. His assignments were for the most part carried out successfully, seemed to be highly thought of, and didn't seem to have any of the emotional baggage that Recker did. There really wasn't anything not to like. But Recker didn't like making decisions on the spot and wanted at least one night to stew it over. Plus, he knew that Jones wouldn't have recommended anyone unless he was certain it was the right pick. And there was a small piece inside him, enjoying making Jones squirm for the night as retaliation for teasing him the way he did.

When Recker got home, Mia had just finished the apartment. He walked in, hoping he wouldn't get the cold shoulder from her for being gone most of the day. As soon as he stepped inside, he was amazed at how different the place looked. It really did feel like he was in someone else's home. Pictures on the wall, flowers on the table, plants by the window, a couple extra lamps that he didn't recall having before. Mia really did do a wonderful job with it, he thought. And with everything finished, he hardly felt any anxiety over the latest changes.

He went over to the wall and stared at the pictures of them together. For the first time he could remember, at least since what happened in London, he finally felt at peace with himself. Looking at the two of them together, their cheeks pressed against each other, he felt like the emptiness he'd been carrying around for so long had gone away. He wasn't longing for Carrie anymore, wasn't wishing circumstances had been different, or that he'd acted in some other way. He was just relishing the fact he had found another woman who loved him unconditionally, much like Carrie did, and that he loved equally as well. For the longest time, he didn't think he'd ever find that feeling again. And for a while, he didn't think he even wanted it. But Mia changed all that.

As he was staring at the pictures on the wall, Mia snuck up behind him and wrapped her arms around his waist. Recker looked back at her and smiled. He turned around and kissed her, hoping she wasn't mad at him. By the warm smile she had planted on her face, he assumed that he wasn't going to get a tongue lashing, or the cold shoulder that he was worried about. As they stared into each other's eyes, Recker put his nose in the air, smelling something good coming from the kitchen.

"What smells so good?"

"Just figured I'd make a little celebration meal for our first night together in our new place," Mia said, her face beaming from ear to ear.

"Oh? What're we having?"

"Figured I'd go Italian tonight. Have some meatballs, spaghetti, lasagna, garlic bread."

"Wow. You're going all out. I don't know if I'll be able to eat all that."

"Smaller portions," she said gleefully, looking down at the folder that he was clutching in his hand. "What's that?"

Recker lifted it up as he explained what it was. "Just some work stuff."

"Oh. So how do you like the apartment?"

"It looks really nice," he said, looking around the room.

"Really? What bothers you about it?"

"Nothing."

"Really? There's nothing that's just eating away at you, nothing that's making you wanna just rip it down and throw it out?" Mia said, sure that there must've been something he didn't like.

"No, really. Everything's fine."

"OK. It's just, I know before you left you were a little uneasy about everything."

"Yeah, I know, that was just me being... stupid. Honestly, everything's fine. I wouldn't change anything. Especially the woman who made it all happen."

Mia couldn't resist planting another kiss on his lips, happy that he seemed to enjoy what she'd done to the place. "Dinner's just about ready," she said, taking him by the hand and leading him into the kitchen.

Recker sat down at the kitchen table as Mia went to the stove and started bringing the food over. She already had plates and utensils set up, along with a nice table-cloth and a candle in the middle. Once she was done putting all the food down, she sat down across from Recker. She couldn't help but notice he looked a little out of it.

"What's the matter? Doesn't it look good?" she said, her eyebrows scrunched down.

Recker shook his head and looked up at her. "No, no, everything looks great. It's just uh…"

"What?"

"I don't think I've ever had a tablecloth on here. Or a candle," Recker said, trying hard to remember. "Come to think of it, I'm not sure if I've ever even eaten on plates here. Except the paper ones."

Mia laughed. "You know, that really doesn't surprise me. You see these plates on the table? They're the only ones I found in the cabinets."

"Oh."

"I'm gonna have to go on a shopping trip. I've noticed you're a little sparse on a few things in here."

"That's the life of a bachelor."

"Well, that's over with now, right?"

"Looks that way," Recker said with a smile. "This might be your last chance to back out you know."

"Why would I want to do that?"

"Well, I'm not wanted by the CIA anymore, but it doesn't extend to the police department. Half of them anyway."

"I'm not really worried."

"You're not? If I'm caught, they could always arrest you as an accomplice or something," Recker said, warning her of the dangers, though it wasn't the first time they'd talked about it.

"And as I've told you before, you getting caught doesn't really worry me."

"It doesn't."

"No, you getting killed… that's what worries me. I

mean, you're out there all alone most of the time, fighting against bad people," Mia said.

She was about to keep going but quickly thought better of it. The last thing she wanted to sound like was a worrywart of a girlfriend. Especially on a day like this, which was a big day for both of them. And she didn't want to be one of those girlfriends who was always nagging or crying about something. She knew Recker didn't need that either. She assumed that the quickest way her fears about Recker dying out would come true, were if his mind was filled with drama at home. Worrying about her instead of focusing on whatever his assignment was. Mia was determined not to do that to him. At least as much as possible. She knew there would eventually be fights or disagreements, as in any relationship, but she was going to try her hardest to not let it be over silly stuff or things that could be avoided. If the unthinkable ever happened, and Recker died out there on the streets, it wouldn't be because of her.

"Well, we're taking some steps to make sure that doesn't happen," Recker said.

"What do you mean?"

"David and I are talking about bringing in another guy. Another Silencer."

Mia laughed at the way he referenced himself. "You just love calling yourself that, don't you?"

Recker smirked. "Yeah, a little bit."

"So, you're really thinking about bringing another person in?"

"That's what the folder's for. David's narrowed it down to one person."

"Why didn't you tell me about this before?" Mia said.

"I didn't know. David just gave it to me today. I didn't realize he was this close."

"So, what do you think?"

"His package looks good," Recker said, admitting to Mia what he wouldn't to Jones.

"You think you'll be able to get along with another guy?"

"Yeah, if he isn't a pompous jerk," Recker said with a laugh. "Besides, maybe that'll free me up at night for more time here with you."

"Well I'm definitely all for that."

"We'll see what happens. But having another person would definitely take some of the strain off."

"I'll be glad when or if it happens," Mia said. "I've always worried about you not having anyone out there watching your back. Especially with some of the situations you wind up getting yourself in."

"You mean the situations other people make me put myself in."

"So, when are you gonna make a decision on this guy?"

"I'll give David the go-ahead tomorrow morning when I go in. I just wanna reread everything to make sure it's the right call."

"Well you've always had great instincts on people. What's your gut say?"

"That he's the guy."

CHAPTER 3

Just as Recker promised, when he came into the office the following morning, he was ready to give Jones his decision. The professor had a tough time sleeping and was awake before the sun came up. He was excited about possibly adding to the team, as well as anxious as he waited for Recker's answer. When Jones first started his search for a new member, he didn't anticipate he'd ever be that thrilled over it. He certainly wasn't that enraptured when the list of candidates first started appearing on his screen. He and Recker had developed a strong friendship and special chemistry. They couldn't do the work that they did without a powerful bond between them. He worried that a new person would possibly disrupt the dynamic that they'd built up. Jones' hopes weren't even that high at first. Finding someone like Recker, who would fit within their team, wouldn't be an easy task. He wasn't sure if it was even doable. It would be like catching lightning in a bottle twice, he thought. But as his search progressed, and he got further along and started diving into some of the candidates' backgrounds, Jones got a little more excited over the prospects of finding that elusive new member.

Jones had whittled the final list of candidates down to three before he selected Haley. In Jones' search parameters, he limited his search to men and women that were single. He assumed those that were married would have a more difficult time in making the move and doing the work that was required. Once the final three were chosen, it really didn't take Jones very long to narrow it down to Haley. As Jones made up the list of the desired attributes, Haley was the only one who checked off all the boxes. He was single, good with firearms, excellent at blending in, and willing to do the most difficult assignments. That was shown by his CIA case record. Haley had been stationed all over the world, Russia, China, North Korea, Africa, the Middle East, Europe, and South America, and spoke several languages. He'd been assigned at various points of his career to take out dictators, drug lords, firearm dealers, and corrupt politicians. His history was as promising as Recker's was when Jones first saw his file.

"You know, I miss the days when I used to beat you into the office," Recker said.

Jones was sitting at the computer typing away, but stopped at Recker's wisecrack. He turned to look at him. "By days, you mean one or two? Because I don't remember any more than that."

"Yeah, well, it's gonna be harder to do now you're living here. Now I won't even have a chance."

"Longing for nostalgia of our days of yesteryear already, are you?"

"What?"

"Nothing. Speaking of nostalgia and things that used to be and are no more, what is your opinion about Mr. Haley?" Jones said.

Recker tossed the folder down on the desk and sighed. Though he was still in favor of adding someone to the team, it was still a new wrinkle. It was another change that he'd have to get used to. Even though he wanted help, he still wondered how he'd react to another guy invading their space, especially when he had a bad enough time watching pictures get hung on the wall of his apartment. He wondered how he'd feel that first time he saw Haley do something that Recker was used to doing. Would he feel grateful, or thankful that he had help? Or would he feel jealous or threatened that someone else was doing his job for him? After a few more moments he came to his senses. He figured he probably wouldn't feel grateful or threatened. After all, there were plenty of bad guys to go around. Recker didn't have the market on them all to himself. There was more out there than he could deal with on his own. And that's what it was all about. Just getting the job done. By whatever means possible.

"I'm good with him." Recker said, finally admitting the truth.

"Hallelujah. I had ideas that you might not ever say what you really thought about him."

"I thought about it."

"I'm sure you did."

"Did you know all along, or did you just come to that conclusion overnight?" Jones said, wondering for his own amusement.

"I had a pretty good idea yesterday."

"Would it have killed you to at least say you were leaning in that direction, instead of making me wonder all day and night? And morning for that matter."

"It might have."

"Somehow I knew you would say that."

"So, what's your plan?" Recker said.

"With?"

"Haley. I mean, I assume you're not gonna just send him an email or a telegram and pitch him our little operation. Right?"

"Of course not. I was planning on seeing him in person and making him an offer."

"When will you be back?"

"When will we be back?"

"We? What do you need me for?"

"Because he's a highly dangerous man that I would like to have some backup on... just in case," Jones said.

"You recruited me alone."

"If you recall, there was some added muscle I hired at first to direct you from the airport. In case you weren't as cooperative as I'd hoped."

"Oh, yeah."

"So, are you ready?"

"For what?" Recker said.

"To go speak to Mr. Haley."

"Right now?"

"Do you have other plans?" Jones said.

"No."

"Well then there's no time like the present, is there?"

"A little notice would've been nice."

"Turnabout is fair play, is it not? You gave me no advanced notice on your thoughts last night. Therefore, I'm giving you none now." Jones flashed a devilish smile.

"You know, sometimes I think my personality may have rubbed off on you too much."

"I know, and it really gives me great pause for concern sometimes."

"How far is this excursion of ours gonna take us?" Recker said. "The one thing missing in his file was where he's at now."

"It's a short trip. He's in Baltimore."

"A nice, short drive."

"We'll be back before dinner. In time for you to hang more curtains tonight."

"Don't start that again. Besides, Mia's working the late shift."

They gathered up a few things from the office and began the drive down to Baltimore. It was only a two-hour drive so they would get there right around lunchtime. Haley was working for a home security systems company, so Jones knew they'd find him at his apartment. Thirty minutes into their drive, Recker had some questions about their upcoming encounter.

"What if he's got other things to do, and he's not there?" Recker said.

"Well then we'll wait until he gets there."

"Easy as that, huh?"

"Easy as that," Jones said.

"Nervous?"

"No. Why?"

"Just wondering. Isn't every day you try to recruit a new member for the squad."

"I've done it before."

"So, what's bothering you?"

"What makes you think something is bothering me?"

"Because I know you. You're not saying much, and you keep looking out the window like you're distracted by something. Unusual for you," Recker said.

"Just thinking about some things."

"You wanna spring it on me?"

"Just thinking about Haley."

"What about him? Having second thoughts already?"

"No. Just a few things I don't understand yet. There's a lot to be learned from his package. You can learn a man's history, his strengths, his weaknesses, but you can't learn everything. Some things you just can't tell until you meet someone and interact with them for a while," Jones said, still looking out the passenger side window.

"What are you getting at?"

"Haley left the CIA two years ago. And in that time, he's had four jobs. Worked in Virginia as a construction worker, in Pittsburgh at an industrial plant, in Delaware as a private security guard, now in Baltimore as a home security guard."

"Can't hold anything down," Recker said.

"I don't understand it. A man with his background, with his record, and he hasn't held onto any of those jobs for longer than six months. He's on his sixth month now with his current job. How do you figure it?"

"My guess? He's unsettled. He's looking for something. He's looking for a home, some sense of belonging. Something to hang his hat on. He's unsatisfied in his work, he's looking for more, and he hasn't found it yet."

"Well if that's true then that may work in our favor," Jones said. "That may make our offer more appealing."

"It probably happens to most guys who've done what we've done. You risk your life for your country and live in continuous danger and, then when it's all over, you find yourself schlepping around a broom somewhere. You feel like your work used to be important. You used to matter. Then you wind up a civilian and find out nobody gives two hoots about you anymore."

"It didn't happen to you."

"I guess I got lucky when I ran into you. Plus, I had something to keep me going. I didn't exactly go out on my own terms like most guys. It's probably also easier for those guys who have a wife or kids, some family to keep their spirits up. Haley doesn't seem to have that going for him."

"No, he doesn't. Never married. No kids. No immediate family to speak of. His father died when he was twelve, and his mother passed away three years ago to cancer. No siblings."

"Didn't he have a couple cousins or something?" Recker said, remembering the file. "Thought I read that in there somewhere."

"Yes, a few cousins down in North Carolina. As far as I can tell he hasn't spoken to them in some time. At least ten years that I could see. Has an aunt and uncle in Denver. Hasn't had contact with them in at least the same amount of time."

"Classic loner."

"I hope not. If he's too much of a loner, he may not be willing to join us," Jones said.

The two of them continued talking about Haley for the rest of the drive. They talked about his background, what would make him so useful to the team, and some of the records that Jones unearthed of him in the CIA. He posed some hypothetical questions to Recker to see how he would have handled some of the situations that Haley found himself in on certain assignments. Most of which Recker said he would have done the same way. They continued talking about Haley the rest of the way to Baltimore, rolling into the city at 11:30 and finding his apartment without much trouble. He had a third-floor unit in a decent area. It wasn't upscale, but it wasn't the bottom of the heap either. Once Recker and Jones got off the elevator on the third floor, they walked to Haley's unit, looking at each other as they stood at the door, making sure neither wanted to turn back before continuing. It was their last chance. Neither did, though. Jones knocked on the door. Haley answered almost at once.

"Can I help you?" Haley said.

"I certainly hope so," Jones replied. "I guess there's really no easy way to get into this, so I'll just get right to the point. We're here to offer you employment."

"Subtle," Recker said.

"I've already got a job."

"Yes, I know. I mean we're here to offer you something meaningful, something you can feel you belong to," Jones said.

"I'm not interested. Thanks."

Haley was about to close the door when Jones knew he had to think of something fast to keep the dialogue flowing. "I know you've been searching for something since you left the CIA," Jones said quickly. "We can help with that." He talked in his normal tone, and Haley stopped the door from closing.

"How do you know I worked for them?" Haley said, looking at the two visitors more closely, thinking that Recker looked like an agent.

"We know everything about you," Jones said. "If we can come in, I can explain everything in greater detail."

"But first, if you could put the gun away that you have hiding behind the door we'd appreciate it," Recker said finally, with a smile.

Jones looked at Recker, then back at Haley, feeling a little uneasy that a gun was being pointed at them if he was correct, which he assumed he was.

"We're not here to hurt you," Jones said, hoping to ease the man's fears.

"If we were we probably wouldn't be standing here asking to come in," Recker said.

Haley knew they were right. If it was somebody gunning for him, they wouldn't give him the courtesy of knocking on the door. They'd shoot first, then exchange pleasantries after he was dead, though it would be one-sided at that point. He tucked the gun inside the belt of his pants and opened the door for his two visitors to enter. Recker and Jones walked into the living room and sat on opposite ends of a couch. Haley sat on a sofa across from them, ready to listen to what they had to say.

"So, are you guys with the agency?" Haley said.

"I used to be," Recker said.

"We're both currently in the public sector. We have nothing to do with any government agencies." Jones watched Haley carefully as he spoke.

"So, what's this offer you were talking about?" Haley said.

"We're here to offer you a job. I assume you're not satisfied with how your life is currently tracking considering you've had four jobs in four different cities in the last two years."

"How do you know all this?"

"Information is something that comes easily to me. Doing something with that information, well, that's where you would come in."

Haley threw his hands up, not sure what his guest was saying to him. "What does all that mean exactly?"

"The short version is that we try to stop bad things happening to good people. We stop robberies, murders, assaults, kidnappings, all before the perpetrators have a chance to enact their crimes. Well, mostly anyway."

"How can you do that?"

"Like I said, information is something that comes easily."

"I don't understand what you need me for. If you get all this information, then why don't you just go to the police?"

"I suppose it's because, technically, my information is gathered through illegal means. Software programs that I've enacted that I learned from my time in the NSA."

"You were in the NSA?"

"At one time. A long time ago. And I learned that there's a lot of good people, innocent people that could be helped by us, that otherwise would just fall through the cracks," Jones said. "Unless we did something about it."

Jones had brought a small computer bag with him and opened it, removing some folders and a couple binders. He put them down on the table in front of Haley for him to look through. It was examples of some of the work he and Recker had done in Philadelphia. News reports, press clippings, the cases they'd worked on, Jones figured that would be more helpful in helping Haley make up his mind than just talking of their exploits. When he first contacted Recker, all he had to go on was faith that their mission could be successful. And all he had was hope that Recker would go along with it. Now, he didn't have to do that. He had real-life examples to show. There were noted cases where it was documented how much of a help they were. But Jones also wasn't going to shy away from admitting the pitfalls either. He was going to be upfront and honest in telling Haley that, though they'd be doing important work, he wouldn't be on the same side as the law. At least in the eyes of the police department.

Haley eagerly looked through the information that was presented to him. He'd already heard of The Silencer, as some of Recker's exploits had become known throughout the east coast. But to sit and have him sitting across from him, looking through some of their files, was something of a thrill for Haley. After hearing of some of their stories through newspaper or TV reports, Haley had always had thoughts of doing something similar. But he didn't know where to start or how to set up an operation like that, so it never got past the idea stage. He didn't have a Jones to oversee anything.

Jones and Recker were giving Haley all the time and space that he needed to go through the things they had provided for him, not eager to rush him into anything. They looked at each other a couple of times, both of them were confident that their approach was working. By the look on Haley's face as he consumed what he was reading, at the very least, seemed intrigued. Eventually, Haley picked his head up to look at his guests, plenty of questions going through his mind.

"I have to admit that I've heard of you guys before," Haley said. "You've kind of made a name for yourself."

"Sometimes too much," Jones said, giving Recker a glance.

"I guess I still have sorta the same question. What do you want with me?"

"Well, our reasons are many. First of which, I'm not that handy with a gun, I'm not a whizz at tailing people, I'm not somebody who excels at close-quarter combat. That's what Mike does. He's the one who's mentioned in all these stories."

"But none of that happens without David," Recker said, making sure Jones got his due and equal share of the credit.

"What I'm good at, is finding the information that these people need help. How I do that is a more complicated answer for another time. But what we're really looking for is another person out in the field, who can help in whatever situation is necessary. We've encountered several situations in the last year or so where another person would have been very useful."

"I'm good, but I can't be everywhere," Recker said.

"And you guys want me to join you?" Haley said, a little awestruck.

"That's why we're here," Jones said.

"I'm sure there are others who may have something better to offer than me."

"I analyzed thousands of files. I couldn't come up with anyone."

"My last couple of years haven't been filled with much to be proud of," Haley said.

"What you need is to be redirected," Jones said. "You need guidance, structure, something important to fight for. We can provide that."

"We can also provide the danger and getting shot at." Recker couldn't resist the quip.

Jones turned to look at his partner, giving him a disapproving look. "By the nature of our work, you will be placed in... difficult situations. That will be unavoidable."

"I'm not afraid to be in danger," Haley said quickly. "If you've seen my file, you know where I've been."

"We know. But I should also point out that even though you'll be doing the right thing, helping people, you will not be a friend to the police department. You will, at some point, become a wanted man. Unfortunately, there is no way around that. Your life as you know it will be over. You'll live and operate in secrecy."

"Living in secrecy's never been an issue for me. What about supplies, guns, stuff like that? Do I bring my own?"

"Whatever you wish. Bring whatever you like. Though I should warn you and point out that Mike has an extensive collection of weapons. Guns will be the least of your worries. Guns, money, vehicles, nothing will be an issue. Everything you will need will be at your disposal."

"Sounds good."

"There's only three things you will need to worry about," Jones said.

"What's that?"

"Successfully completing your assignment, staying out of public view as much as possible, and staying alive."

"Three things that aren't an issue for me."

"Now, we have had our fair share of publicity for whatever reasons, but we try to avoid being put in the spotlight. The more media coverage we get, the more police attention we receive as well. We obviously would rather not have either."

"Works for me. I couldn't care less about attention," Haley said, seemingly on board with the proposal.

"So far, this has been a two-man operation. We have no egos, no ulterior motives, nothing else matters except helping those who need it."

"I don't have an ego to check. I'm all about doing whatever's needed. I've always been a team player."

"That's one of the reasons we're here," Jones said. "Your file indicates you'd fit in."

"Would we work as a pair or separately?"

"Sometimes both. It all depends on the type of case and how many we're working. Everything's on the table."

As Jones continued talking about their operation, Haley kept looking through the files and documents that were laid out on the table. He was trying to soak in as much as possible. Though he tried not to show it too much outwardly, Haley was ready to burst out of his seat to accept the proposal. He had nothing there that was holding him back. And it seemed like the perfect opportunity to get back in the game. This was the type of work he enjoyed, and he knew he was good at. Since leaving the CIA, he'd been searching for something to fill the void. This would be the chance he was looking for to feel like his work mattered again.

"What made you leave the agency?" Recker said. "I didn't see anything mentioned in your file. You could've stayed on a few more years if you wanted."

"Yeah. There was a woman. A girlfriend," Haley said, looking depressed the moment he thought about her.

"Well, that's eerily familiar," Jones said.

"What happened?" Recker said.

"Mike, that's not our business."

"No, it's fine," Haley said. "I'd rather have everything out on the table with you guys. I'm not hiding anything. I met a girl, and I fell in love with her. Was with her for a few years. But she got tired of the frequent missions which meant I was out of the country all the time. So, I agreed to leave the agency to preserve our relationship."

"I guess things went sideways?" Recker said.

"Yeah, you could say that. I was out of the country for about two months on my final assignment. When I came back, she was gone."

"She just left you?"

"Yeah. At first, I tried to look for her. Took a job down in Virginia to get by while I was searching. Then, after about six months, I found her. I used some contacts of mine from the CIA and found her living in Pittsburgh. So, I went there."

"And?" Jones said.

"She was with another man. She apparently met him even before I gave my notice," Haley said. "So, then I just kind of bounced around at a couple jobs till I wound up here."

"And you didn't kill either of them?" Recker said, half-jokingly.

Haley laughed. "No. Not that I didn't have thoughts

about it. But, no, they're both living, safe and sound, happy as can be I guess."

"Pity."

They talked for another couple of hours, Jones continuing to give Haley the rundown about how their operation worked, what would be expected, and what, if anything, Haley needed. Once they were finished, Jones started picking the papers off the table, and put them back in his computer bag. He looked at the time and figured they needed to be getting back to Philadelphia. It was already past three.

"Well, we should be heading home," Jones said, reaching into his bag for a business card and handing it to Haley. "Take a few days to make your decision. Think about it. I'd appreciate a phone call when you've made up your mind. Either way."

Haley took it and looked at it briefly, before handing it back to Jones. "I don't need this. And I don't need a few days to think about it. I'm in," Haley said happily.

"Are you sure?"

"Definitely. I've got nothing keeping me here. This is the type of work I'm made to do. This is what I'm good at."

"Just to be clear, we're looking for someone for the long term. We're not interested in someone who's only going to stick around a few months or so before looking for something else."

"That's not a problem. I'll be in it for the long haul. You don't have to worry about me," Haley said, knowing they had fears over his recent work history. "These last couple years with those other jobs, I was just trying to fit in somewhere. This is what I need."

Jones looked at Recker, who nodded his head in approval.

"Well then, it looks like we have a deal," Jones said.

"Welcome aboard," Recker said, shaking Haley's hand.

"What do you need me to do first?"

"Take care of whatever you need to do here. Pack up, quit your job, take care of any bills or anything else you have," Jones said. "Make sure there's no outstanding issues that someone might track you down for."

"I can let my job know today. Won't take me long to pack. A day at the most. I can be up in Philly by tomorrow night."

"How's your car?"

"My car?"

"Yes, does it run OK?"

"Well, it's got about a hundred thousand miles on it, but I haven't really had many issues with it. Why?"

"Make sure you're still here tomorrow morning," Jones said. "You'll be getting a delivery."

ALSO BY MIKE RYAN

Continue reading the next book in The Silencer Series, Double Tap.

Other Books:

The Extractor Series

The Cain Series

The Eliminator Series

The Ghost Series

The Brandon Hall Series

The Cari Porter Series

A Dangerous Man

The Last Job

The Crew

ABOUT THE AUTHOR

Mike Ryan is a USA Today Bestselling Author. He lives in Pennsylvania with his wife, and four children. He's the author of the bestselling Silencer Series, as well as many others. Visit his website at www.mikeryanbooks.com to find out more about his books, and sign up for his newsletter. You can also interact with Mike via Facebook, and Instagram.

www.ingramcontent.com/pod-product-compliance
Lightning Source LLC
Chambersburg PA
CBHW070550310726

48982CB00011B/1533/J